SEVEN WAYS TO KILL A CAT

Born in Buenos Aires in 1975, Matías Néspolo studied literature, going on to write poems, short stories, journalism and then *Seven Ways to Kill a Cat*, his acclaimed first novel. He has been living in Barcelona since 2001 and, in 2010, was selected by *Granta* as one of their best young contemporary Spanish-language novelists.

MATÍAS NÉSPOLO

Seven Ways to Kill a Cat

TRANSLATED FROM THE SPANISH BY
Frank Wynne

VINTAGE BOOKS
London

Published by Vintage 2012

2 4 6 8 10 9 7 5 3 1

First published in Great Britain in 2011 by
Harvill Secker

Vintage
Random House, 20 Vauxhall Bridge Road,
London SW1V 2SA

www.vintage-books.co.uk

Addresses for companies within The Random House Group Limited
can be found at: www.randomhouse.co.uk/offices.htm

The Random House Group Limited Reg. No. 954009

A CIP catalogue record for this book
is available from the British Library

ISBN 9780099552383

This book has been selected to receive financial assistance from English
PEN's Writers in Translation programme supported by Bloomberg.
English PEN exists to promote literature and its understanding, uphold
writers' freedoms around the world, campaign against the persecution
and imprisonment of writers for stating their views, and promote the
friendly co-operation of writers and free exchange of ideas

Recommended by pen

The Random House Group Limited supports The Forest Stewardship
Council (FSC®), the leading international forest certification
organisation. All our titles that are printed on FSC®
certified paper carry the FSC logo. FSC is the only forest certification scheme endorsed
by the leading environmental organisations, including Greenpeace.
Our paper procurement policy can be found at:
www.randomhouse.co.uk/environment

Printed in Great Britain by Clays Ltd, St Ives plc

TRANSLATOR'S NOTE

One of the challenges in any translation is preserving a sense of place, affording the reader a glimpse of the foreign, of another life, another culture.

The Buenos Aires of *Seven Ways to Kill a Cat* is not simply a place, it is a patchwork of smells and tastes and especially sounds since Matías Néspolo does not *describe* this world but conjures it through dialogue, idiom and slang. Slang varies from country to country, from city to city, even from town to town. More than meaning, it has a music and an attitude; translating it, taming it can risk making what is alien too familiar.

In trying to capture the crackling energy of these voices, the vernacular of drugs and guns and sex, I felt there was a danger that these street kids from Buenos Aires might sound as though they were from south London (or east Baltimore), so I have chosen to keep elements of the original which I hope can be easily understood in context. Since I could not imagine Gringo addressing his friends as 'mate', 'buddy', 'bro' or 'brah', I borrowed from Spanish the many words for friend – *socio* (partner), *loco* (madman), *viejo* (old friend), *compañero* (comrade), *pibe* (kid) and the ubiquitous Argentinian interjection *che* (which can translate as 'man' or simply as 'hey!') which famously gave Ernesto Guevara his nickname.

Many characters in the book are also only ever referred to by their nicknames and these, too, I left unchanged, deciding that, on balance, more would be lost than gained by having characters called Bandy-legs (*El Chueco*), Blondie (*Gringo*), Babyface (*El Jetita*) and The Jellyfish (*El Medusa*).

Lastly, there are the cultural trappings that have no equivalents – foodstuffs like *morcilla* (a blood sausage utterly unlike black pudding), *alfajores* (chocolate-covered sandwich biscuits filled with quince jelly or caramel), to say nothing of the complex ritual of making and drinking *mate* (carefully prepared from bitter *yerba buena* leaves in a hollow gourd, often ornately carved and with a silver rim, and drunk through a *bombilla* – a long metal straw). *Mate* is not simply a drink like coffee or tea, but a crucial ritual of friendship and bonding.

The Buenos Aires where Gringo and his friends live is not the city of broad avenues, baroque cemeteries, the *Casa Rosada* and Tango, but one that visitors and indeed most *porteños* never see: neighbourhoods like Zavaleta to the south of the city, between shantytowns 21 and 24, where families live in makeshift shacks without water or electricity surrounded by crumbling buildings and new apartment blocks, areas blighted by poverty, petty crime and *paco* (a cheap cocaine paste like crack). But these are also places that crackle with extraordinary energy, with danger, with *cumbia* music and with hope. Welcome to the barrio.

Frank Wynne

SEVEN WAYS TO KILL A CAT

TWO WAYS

'There's seven ways to kill a cat,' Chueco says, stroking the animal Ernestina's kid just brought him, and giving me a sly wink.

He cradles it in his left arm and strokes its head, leaning over like he's trying to protect it, then jerks back as it lashes out. I hear a sound like a dead branch snapping and Chueco lifts the shuddering cat by the scruff of its neck. The head is lolling, the paws rigid. It stops moving.

'But when it comes down to it, there's only two ways,' he goes on like he's teaching a class. 'In a civilised fashion, or like a fucking savage.'

'Don't tell me. That was savage?' I say to wind him up.

'No, *viejo*, that was civilised. This way the kitty doesn't suffer because . . .' He lets the sentence trail off and laughs. When he laughs, he screws up his face so he looks like an old woman in pain. He looks so ridiculous, I laugh too. Not much, just a bit. Just enough to convince myself this thing I'm staring at isn't a cat any more. It's food, a gift from God. I haven't had meat in over a week and I'm fucking sick of cornmeal mush – I figure Chueco is too – or the weevil-infested rice we get free from a grocer up in Zavaleta and the plums we steal from the garden of the old Portuguese guy, Oliveira.

Chueco holds the cat by the hind legs so its head is hanging down. With a quick backhand flick of his knife, he slits its throat, and nudges a tin can under the head with his foot to collect the blood.

'What the fuck are you going to do, make *morcilla*?' I say.

'What does it look like?' he says. I don't know if he's taking the piss or if he's really planning on using the blood to make black pudding, so I don't say anything. I just watch him, let him get on with it.

With a deep slash, he slits the cat open and guts it. The entrails spill into the can. Chueco moves quickly, skilfully. He looks like a pro.

'Now for the tricky bit,' he says, jerking the tip of the blade at me, his eyes half closed.

He cuts off the tail and starts to cut around the paws, following the curve of the joint.

'It's a bit like stripping electric wire,' he explains, 'except it's got fur obviously, and it's thicker. Bit like Fat Farías's finger.'

'Fat Farías! There's a lot of fucking meat on him . . . Why don't we just butcher him?' I'm joking, but Chueco gets a serious look and I see a gleam in those beady little eyes.

'Forget butchering him! We should fleece the fat fucker of all that cash he's got stashed away.'

'What are you talking about? Farías hasn't got two pesos to rub together, he's as fucked as everyone else round here. You know he's in deep shit with his suppliers. If things don't pick up, he's not even going to have beer to sell in that dive of his.'

'He's in the shit because he's a stingy fucker, forever crawling to God and the Holy Virgin Mary. I'm telling you, Gringo, Farías has a fat wad of cash stashed somewhere.'

'*Yeah, in the bank maybe,*' I'm about to say but I bite my tongue. Stupid fucking thing to say. Since the exchange rate tanked last September, nobody puts money in a bank. Anyone with serious cash gets it out of the country, but that wouldn't include Farías, 'El Gordo'. Most people who've got a little bit put aside just stuff it under the mattress.

While I'm thinking this, Chueco cuts along the inside of the cat's hind paws, pulls the skin back like he's peeling a salami, grips the two flaps and yanks hard, turning it inside out like a sock. The pelt now hangs from the front paws like a doll's coat, the fur on the inside. Chueco cuts it away.

'In-fucking-credible. Watch and learn, Gringo,' he says, flinging the skin at my head. 'You're skinning the next one.'

I duck, but I don't say anything. The skin flops to the ground about four feet away. When I turn, I see Ernestina's kid, Quique, quietly creeping over to it. He prods it with a stick. The fur is just a ball of dirt and blood.

'Give it a good wash and dry it in the sun,' I tell him. 'It'll make a bag. Or give it to your baby sister for her doll.'

Quique stares at me, mouth open. The kid's clueless. He picks up the skin, shakes it and, seeing the shape, starts giggling to himself, like when he was little and used to laugh at everything. These days, he comes up to my shoulder, but I still think of him as a kid.

Chueco keeps working away. With the point of the knife, he removes the lungs and tosses them into the can. Then he goes into the shack where he lives, comes out with a rag, wipes his hands and cleans the blade of the knife. He lights a cigarette, raises his eyebrows and looks at me questioningly.

I spark up a *negro* myself and look at the cat hanging from a nail on the wall. Without the skin it looks like rabbit – like hare, actually. I suddenly remember how Mamina, my grandmother, used to cook hare when I was a kid. Cousin Toni used to

bring them round before he sold his shotgun. I
can't stop myself.

'Why don't we make a stew?'

'Fuck, no! Slap it on a grill, flip it over and it's
done.'

'Whatever you say, *socio*.'

'We grill it,' he says firmly. He likes to think he's
in charge. And I let him.

'Fair enough, I'll get a fire going.'

'Yeah, you do that. Hey, kid?' He turns to
Quique who's still standing, watching everything.
'What the fuck you still doing here?'

'*Mamá* said if there's any left over could we have
a bit for Sultán,' he says, 'because he's always
whining.'

'A little something for the señora's doggy?'
Chueco says, putting on a squeaky voice. 'Sure!' I
don't know why, but he can't stand the sight of
Ernestina.

'Here, kid.' He holds out the can of entrails. 'You
can have this.'

Quique shuffles away, the fur in one hand and
the tin can in the other. His shoes are falling off,
they've got no laces and they're two sizes too big
for him. I watch him leave as I squat down to put
a match to some crumpled pieces of paper and add
little bits of wood from an old drawer I've just
smashed up.

'You stingy fucking bastard,' I say to Chueco.

5

'Why didn't you give him a bit of the meat?'

Chueco looks at me, clicks his tongue, takes a last drag on his cigarette then stubs it out.

'If he wanted some, he should have asked instead of pissing about. He said he wanted dog food, so that's what he got. Anyway, the offal is delicious. You can make a fantastic stew out of it.'

I keep working on the fire. I'm pretty sure Quique's thing about his *mamá* needing to feed the dog was bullshit. The kid just wanted a bit of meat for himself. I don't say this to Chueco, no point winding him up, but not saying anything winds him up anyway because he keeps trying to justify himself.

'Besides, the kid's a fucking freak. His *mamá* could have told him to go catch their own cat instead of taking ours. But oh no! Señora Ernestina doesn't eat cat, the old bitch!'

'Maybe he doesn't know how to kill and butcher it.'

'Well, he can learn, *viejo*, or he can go fuck himself.'

BOTTLING POISON

The beer's warm. Looks more like milkshake than beer – two parts foam to one part liquid. But I can't face an argument, so I drink it anyway. Besides, Fat Farías is a stingy bastard. If I make him pull a fresh one with less foam, he'll want me to shell out and I don't have a peso.

Chueco comes in poker-faced and pale, swaggers over to my table and shouts, 'Bottle of rotgut red, Gordo!'

He sits down and stares at me. Eyes wide. Blank. Expressionless. Fat Farías comes over carrying the bottle and a glass in the same hand. Chueco goes on.

'*Qué onda*, Gringuito?' He tilts his head and grins like a maniac. He makes like he's chilled, but it's forced. It's all an act.

'Fine, good . . .' I say, giving him the same deranged grin. Let's see what he says. He's making me nervous. He blinks, keeping his eyes closed a split second longer than necessary. Chueco does that sometimes. It's like a card player's tic, it's hard to spot but I notice it. I just don't know what the fuck it means.

Farías plonks the glass down on the table with a bang, tilts the bottle, but before he pours, he barks, 'That'll be two pesos!'

'Chill, Gordo,' El Chueco says. 'What's with you?' He's trying to be sarcastic but he botches it. He's harder than a rock.

'First things first,' Fat Farías says.

'Fuck sake, don't sweat it, just pour. It's all cool.'

On the table next to the glass is a fifty-peso note. I don't know where it came from.

Fat Farías picks it up and fills Chueco's glass to the brim.

'Leave the bottle,' Chueco says, pulling a face, not even looking at him.

Fat Farías picks up on the snub.

'Fuck you,' he lets fly. 'That's all I need, another little runt trying to make like a gangster. Who did you rip off? Your *mamá*?'

'Little bit of respect there, Gordo, wouldn't want things to kick off . . .'

'Who's going to do the kicking? You, you legless little runt?' Fat Farías chucks the change on the table and stomps back to the bar choking back a laugh with a cough.

'Yeah, go ahead and laugh,' Chueco mutters through his teeth. 'You'll be crying soon enough.'

He winks at me and knocks back the glass of wine. I'm not going to step into the firing line, so I just give him the same crazed grin he gave me when he showed up.

'So, what's been happening, Gringo?'

'What the fuck is with you? Want to tell me where you got a fifty-peso note?'

'Don't sweat it, it's snide. Relax, I'll fill you in later.'

I finish my beer. Light a cigarette. Chueco holds up two fingers asking for the cigarette I didn't offer. I tap the bottom of the pack, shake one out and grudgingly give it to him.

'That's better, *compañero*. No need to be tight with the merchandise.'

Chueco fills his glass again and pours some into my beer glass. The wine brings the beer foam from the bottom to the surface.

'What the fuck you doing?' I shout.

'Don't be such a punk bitch, just drink it,' he says.

I'm pissed off by his tone, but he's got a point – this stuff's not rotgut, it's fucking rat poison. Doesn't matter if you mix it with beer or Coke or piss, it's bitter as carob juice. What's weird is the bottle's legit, but I'm guessing it didn't come with this cat's piss in it. Explains why Fat Farías always uncorks wine at the bar before bringing it over.

I figure the fat fucker has a stash of cheap wine

in his cellar – the shit that comes in twenty-litre barrels – and bottles it behind the bar. Not that I give a fuck if he wants to bottle his own wine. But the day Fat Farías tries to make the spirits go a bit further and gets his hand on the wrong kind of alcohol, he'll probably fucking kill someone. I'm guessing he knows fuck all about chemistry. Not that I do, but I know the difference between the surgical alcohol you buy at the chemist and the alcohol fuel they sell in barrels down the hardware store. One gets you wasted, the other wastes you. Wouldn't be the first time someone pulled a stunt like that in the barrio.

I'm thinking all this while I'm sipping my poison, and before I've even finished Chueco's pouring me another. The fucker hasn't said a word, and it doesn't look like he's going to any time soon.

'Hey,' I say, 'that fat fucker's riding for a fall –'

'Finish the bottle with me. I've got a little business proposition for you.'

The minutes pass and still Chueco says nothing. Every now and then he glances back at the bar. Farías knows he's doing it, but he obviously thinks he got one over on us because he's got this big shit-eating grin. And whenever Chueco isn't looking, he's pointing and laughing with the other guys at the bar. Chueco's got his back to them and he's deep in his own shit, so he doesn't notice and I'm not about to say anything. I don't want him kicking off.

10

'So, talk or I'm gone.'

Chueco drains his glass, glances round at the bar, then turns and stares out the window at the street. Finally, he leans back in his chair and looks at me.

'Give us a cigarette before you go then. Probably for the best. You haven't got the balls for what I've got planned.'

'You calling me chickenshit?' I say, and the urge to put my fist through his face makes me sound tense, which just makes me more furious because suddenly I realise it's a set-up. Clever. But I've put myself out there now, I can't back down.

'I'm not calling anyone anything,' he says soberly. 'Just telling it like it is.'

'When?'

'Tonight. But right now I'm not sure. I mean, I'd like you as my backup, but if you're just going to tag along with your tail between your legs don't bother.'

'What the fuck do you take me for, Chueco? You looking for a smack in the mouth?' It's not a threat, it's an invitation for him to say something, give me a good reason to smash his face. But he's a crafty fucker, he knows me too well. He's got what he wanted. So he just gives a soft laugh and says nothing. I clench my fists and walk out, my heart hammering in my temples.

CODE VIOLATION

In the split second between Fat Farías putting the key in the lock and turning it, and the crowbar hitting the back of his head, which slams against the metal door and pushes it open, a thousand different thoughts burn through my brain. I'm off my face on coke. Chueco's fifty-peso bill might have been dud, but it was real enough to get us three grams of *merca*, and we've already snorted the lot.

I think: what'll happen if Farías recognises us? Chueco says we'll be fine, but with him you never know. Not that I'd give a shit if we killed the fat bastard, but then I think about Yanina, Farías's daughter. Supposedly she's out dancing down at the local *cumbia* club like every Thursday – that's why the job has to be tonight – but what if she's inside watching TV? And even if she's not, what if this shit goes bad? Farías might be a son of a bitch but he treats that kid like a princess. Yani's mother died a couple of years ago and I don't fancy leaving

the kid an orphan. I say 'kid', but these days
Yanina's got one hell of a body on her. Far as I
know, she hasn't got any other relatives. If anything
goes wrong and she's left to look after the bar on
her own, she'll be eaten alive.

I think: what if someone sees us? I jerk my head
round, check no one's watching before I whack
Farías. Chueco's never had a moral code. Now I
don't either. But in the barrio, there is a code
everyone lives by: you don't shit on your own
doorstep. Any shit that goes down in the barrio is
generally the work of some dumb fuck who
accidentally wandered onto our turf. The code in
the barrio makes sense. Least you know when you
send your kid down the bakery, your neighbour's
not going to mug him, because if he does he won't
live long enough to brag about it. And it means
you're not going to jump that girl walking down an
alley at night because you don't want someone else
fucking your wife or your sister or your daughter.

I can't see anyone, but you never know. In the
darkness, there are thousands of restless eyes. All
it takes is one person looking this way and we're
fucked. Well and truly fucked. Because we'd be
better off getting beat down by the Feds than
having the people round here remind us of the
code.

As Farías's head slams into the metal door, time
starts up again And I stop thinking.

'Come on, come on, move it . . .' Chueco hisses, trying to push Farías's body inside. When I whacked him, he keeled over in the doorway. I step over the body, grab his shoulders and haul him inside. Chueco closes the door. A dog is barking somewhere and I can barely hear Fat Farías's hoarse moan. He's half conscious. Chueco wraps his head in a burlap bag he got from fuck knows where. He always comes prepared. He takes off his belt and lashes Farías's hands behind his back.

I tiptoe down the corridor. The place is dark, deserted. I come to some sort of living room. The glow from the street lights streams through the half-closed venetian blinds. I turn a light on. A table, three chairs, a television balanced on a plastic beer crate, and everywhere you look, there's rubbish.

Chueco comes in and starts poking around. There's nowhere much in here to hide any cash. After couple of minutes, we move on to the kitchen. The place is filthy: dirty dishes, cockroaches, burnt saucepans. There are no doors on the cupboards or the cabinets under the counter. We don't need to touch them to see what's inside – just as well since I'm figuring they haven't been cleaned since Yani's mother died. And probably not for a couple of years before that. The fridge is empty, maybe broken. Chueco checks it out, then starts opening the pots and jars on the shelves. Pasta, beans, *mate*, sugar . . .

'What the fuck are you doing?' I hiss.

'What's it look like, *dumbfuck*? Misers always stash their cash in weird places. Don't you know anything?'

When Chueco starts making like he knows everything, I want to strangle the bastard, but I don't say anything. Anyway, maybe he's right. Probably best to check everywhere. I leave him to it and head into the next room. It's Yanina's room. I can tell from the photos pinned on the walls and the clothes strewn all over on the floor: a cotton blouse, a bra and a pair of Lycra shorts. I pick up the shorts, stretch them, and picturing her tight arse in them gives me a fucking hard-on. I check the wardrobe, turn the bed over, rummage through the drawers in the bedside table. I know there's no way Farías's money is in here, but since Chueco's being thorough searching the kitchen, I figure it's a good excuse for me to go through Yanina's stuff.

Her room is a tip too, but everything in it is impregnated with the smell of her. I like it. In a drawer in the dressing table, among the lipsticks, the make-up and the nail polish, I find a spliff and tuck it behind my ear. There's a bunch of photos and papers in the other drawers and I'm reading them when Chueco starts shouting and distracts me.

15

'What did I tell you?! That *hijo de puta*– come and see this – it's fucking unbelievable.' He sounds genuinely surprised. 'It's not even like Gordo works in a bank.'

I find him in Fat Farías's bedroom looking so amazed it's like he's dislocated his jaw.

'It's just like in the movies, Gringo. I can't fucking believe it!'

'What the fuck are you talking about?' I hate it when he's all mysterious, it makes me nervous. 'Did you find the cash?'

'Look,' he says, pointing to the built-in wardrobe, the mesh screen door covered in fly shit.

He rips it open, pushes Fat Farías's clothes along the rail and suddenly I see what's got him all worked up. At the back of the wardrobe there's a safe – one of those old green safes with a little black dial where you put in the combination and all that shit. I glance over at Chueco, and when I see the look of misery on his face, all my tension is released and I burst out laughing.

'What the fuck you giggling at, you moron? What are we supposed to do now?'

I can't say anything. I'm holding my sides, laughing so hard I feel like I'm about to dislocate something. As I wipe tears from my face, I hear a metallic twang I recognise. It's the spring of his flick knife.

'Only one thing for it, we'll have to wake up

our fat friend and persuade him to give us the combination,' he says, running his thumb along the blade, and the almost affectionate tone of his voice scares the shit out of me.

'Hold up, you mad fucker. Look at this thing.' I rap on the safe with my knuckles. 'Can't you see it's a piece of shit?'

It sounds like a biscuit tin, which surprises even me. The door's rusted along the bottom, at the top and around the lock itself, which has one of those big handles you get on bank vaults. It's a Mickey Mouse safe. A toy for gullible misers. The sort of thing a kid would pull apart just to see how it works.

Without a word, I retrace my steps, pick up the crowbar I whacked Farías with and head back into the bedroom. Chueco is pale. He opens his mouth but he doesn't say anything. I signal for him to stand back. I give the handle a vicious clout and it comes loose from the rust-eaten door. I jiggle it until it comes off, blow into the hole, some flakes of rust flutter out, and I slip my fingers inside. Using a fingernail I release the catch and the safe opens. Simple as. Like I've been doing this shit my whole life.

I don't have time to wonder how I came up with this brainwave because Chueco has already got both hands in the safe and is pulling everything out: old documents, invoices, receipt books, porn mags, mortgage deeds, leaflets from wine merchants and meat suppliers from years back and, lastly, a shoebox tied with string.

'Bingo . . .' Chueco says, cutting the string with his flick knife.

He takes off the lid and banknotes in every colour of the rainbow spill out – blue, brown, green, red, purple . . . They've all got lots of zeros and they all bear the face of El Libertador. We stand there, staring at them like idiots. I remember notes like this, and I'm sure Chueco does. A brown one used to buy you a bag of popcorn, for a blue one you could get a bottle of Coke. If you had a red one, you could have a blowout. *Pesos ley*, they were called back in the late 1970s. They haven't been in circulation for nearly fifteen years.

Hands shaking, Chueco tips out the contents of the box, and when he sees there's no legal tender, he starts cursing and swearing, his voice quavering and shrill like he's about to cry any minute.

'Don't fuck about,' I warn him. 'Someone'll hear us.'

This just makes it worse. He starts screaming and lashing out, kicking anything within reach.

'Chueco, come on, we need to get out of here. It's over.'

He's not listening. I grab him by the shoulders and push him towards the door. When he sees Fat Farías lying at the far end of the corridor, his rage boils up again. He gives him a savage running kick that lifts the fat bastard off the ground, for all his weight. Farías seems half dead. He barely whimpers now as Chueco lays into him.

'Stop! Chueco, stop! Fucking animal!' I shout and plant myself between his boot and Farías's head.

I bend down and check Farías over. There's a roll of bills in his shirt pocket. It's not much, but at least it's real money.

'Come on,' I say, 'let's get the hell out of here.'

'No, wait,' Chueco says. 'I'm confiscating this too.' He rips off Fat Farías's wristwatch – a Citizen that's at least ten years old – and waves it under my nose. His eyes are shining now, and the moron is laughing.

'Come on,' I shout, 'let's do one.'

A LITTLE CHAT

'Gringo!'

'Huh . . . ?'

'Gringo! Gringooo!'

Someone's shaking my shoulder.

'What? What is it?'

'Gringo!'

I open my eyes. It's Quique.

'What you doing here? Where's Mamina?'

'She's outside having a chat with my old woman.'

Unwillingly I crawl out of bed and start getting dressed. It's hot. The window's open. The sun's already high and hammering down hard. Quique is yakking away but I'm not listening. My brain is a fog. I put on some slippers and head into the bathroom. The cold water brings me round a bit. I'm awake now.

'Shouldn't you be in school?' I ask.

Quique looks at me pleadingly.

'No school today. Teachers' strike.'

'You had breakfast?' I say, wandering into the kitchen.

Quique trots after me like a lapdog. He's been following me around for days now – I've only just noticed.

'You had breakfast?' I ask again, putting the kettle on the hotplate.

'Yeah . . .' He doesn't sound convinced.

The water boils. I brew up some strong *mate*. Quique sits at the kitchen table watching me. I put the two *mate*s on the table, look to see if there's any bread but there isn't, but I do find a packet of biscuits with three left. I chuck the kid two of them, wolf the other one and sit down. Quique blows on the steaming *mate*, carefully dunks the first biscuit and eats it slowly. He repeats the operation with the second biscuit. When he's finished, he blows on the *mate* again and takes a sip. He squeezes his eyes shut and swears.

'Fuck sake, I just burnt my balls. It's fucking scalding.'

'Just like it should be,' I say.

I like the little runt. He's a good kid.

He keeps on blowing and tries again. This time he pulls a face.

'What's up, *viejo*?' I say.

'Got any sugar?'

'My apologies, sir,' I say with a bow.

Quique looks at me warily, but I'm not taking

the piss – I forgot the sugar because I don't take any. I get up and fetch a spoon and a couple of those little sachets I steal for Mamina from McDonald's whenever I pass one. She likes her *mate* sweet. Really sweet.

Quique toys with the sachet for a second or two, thanks me with a nod, then rips it open and tips in the sugar. He stirs it carefully, like it's some explosive mixture. We drink in silence.

When he's done, he tosses down the spoon and gets up.

'So? We going, or what?'

'Where?'

'Shit, *loco*, I told you already!' He's angry now.

Nobody likes having to repeat stuff because someone couldn't be bothered to listen. Not even kids. Especially not Quique. From the way he moves, his silences, even his expression, it's like he's a miniature adult. Like he's been forced to grow up before his time.

I pat him on the back. 'So where was it we were going to go, champ?' I ask again. Truth is I've got no idea. He probably told me while I was getting dressed but it didn't register.

'Down the dump, collecting cardboard. El Chelo lent me his cart. He's not going down there today, something to do with the march, the teachers' strike and all that shit.'

'I can't,' I lie. 'I've got stuff on.'

He looks up at me with big round eyes, disappointed. Either he's pissed at me, or he really needs the few centavos he'll get for twenty kilos of paper. Both probably.

'Hey . . . don't take it like that, *che*. It's no big deal. I mean, it's not worth it, is it, slogging your guts out all day for a couple of pesos . . . ?

Quique sighs, stares into the distance. It's like he's not there. I stuff my hands in my pockets, feel the roll of bills in the right-hand one. I've got some cash. I peel off a five-peso note and hold it out.

'Here, go buy yourself something . . . and make the most of your day off.'

Quique stares, open-mouthed, suspicious.

'Thanks, Gringo,' he says and he's off like a shot.

'Hey, get something for your kid sister!' I shout as he disappears through the strip curtain onto the street.

I amble after him. Outside, Grandma is leaning on her broom chatting to Ernestina.

'Hey, Mamina, how are you this morning?'

Ernestina's too busy shouting after Quique to register I'm there. But the kid's already too far away to be able to hear.

'Good, good, *m'hijo*,' she says and gives me a wrinkly smile, her face screwed up like a raisin.

Ernestina flashes me a poor excuse for a smile then goes back to talking to Mamina. Quique's mother is not looking after herself these days. She's aged a lot, she's really pale and she's lost a ton of weight. Her tits have gone south and it looks like her smile's gone with them. You'd never know she used to be wild sexy Ernestina who turned the head of every man in the barrio.

I light a cigarette. Seeing that I'm still staring at her, Ernestina says to me, 'I suppose you've heard?'

'Heard what?' I say.

Ernestina doesn't answer, she goes back to telling Mamina the story, the two of them huddled together gossiping in low voices. I stand there eavesdropping.

'. . . someone mugged Farías last night, nearly killed him. The paramedics had to rush him to hospital in an ambulance. Fractured his skull, they did, and broke a couple of ribs. A couple of lads, people are saying, delinquents, junkies. Did anyone see them? Possibly. It couldn't be any of the boys from the barrio, it must be someone who came in from Zavaleta. It's terrible. It's not safe to walk the streets these days. Rubén says when he tracks them down, he's going to shoot them where they stand. What about the daughter? She wasn't in the house, thank God.'

I listen intently, not saying anything, not reacting. I don't know how I'm even supposed to react: surprise, anger, curiosity, indifference . . . ? The whole thing sounds so unreal, it's like it's got nothing to do with me. Honestly.

I know I should be worried when Rubén's name comes up, but it just rolls off me. Rubén runs the local scrapyard, but far as I know he doesn't go around strapped. Even if he did, he's hardly the sort of guy to make you shit your pants. But he's a man of his word: if Rubén says he'll do something, he does it. That's why even the Feds round here respect him. He never fucks them over, except maybe in the dodgy business deals they've got going.

What *does* worry me is the fact that Rubén's tight with El Jetita. Now El Jetita really is one dangerous *hijo de puta*. He's the local drugs lord, his crew handles all the weed and the *merca* in the barrio. If Rubén manages to convince El Jetita to sign up for this crusade to cap the guys who beat up Fat Farías, we're screwed. No two ways.

Thing is, I can't work out why Rubén would give a flying fuck about Farías. Maybe he's developed a taste for the rat poison he serves. Or maybe he's trying to make himself look like an upstanding citizen so he can get in good with someone. But I doubt that. It's too complicated for something Rubén would come up with. There's only two possible reasons for Rubén to get mixed up in something like this: either something's in it for him, or it's sheer blind rage. Problem is, I can't see what could possibly be in this for Rubén, but I can't see why he'd be all fired up either. Finding out who whacked a lowlife like Fat Farías isn't the sort

25

of thing to get people round here worked up. Especially not Rubén.

Obviously there's the whole barrio 'code of honour' thing, but I don't think it's about that. There's something here that doesn't fit. Something stinks. Stinks like a dead cat . . .

'I'm heading out, Mamina. You need anything . . .' I say slyly as I slip a couple of big bills into the pocket of her apron, 'apart from money?'

'How about a kiss, my little Gringo?' she says, sweet-talking me.

I give her a kiss; even give her a quick hug. Something about the tone of her voice bugs me. It's weird, but when she called me *Gringo*, it's like she was talking to someone else. At least that's how it sounded.

Gringo's not actually my name, but it might as well be. I haven't got another one. It's what Mamina has called me ever since I was a kid. She says it's because my hair used to be almost blond. No point getting bent out of shape about it. I'm Gringo, even if it's not my name.

Mamina's not actually my grandmother either, but she might as well be. I haven't got another one. She raised *mamá*, and after *mamá* disappeared she raised me. She's not my mother's real mother. But there's no point getting bent out of shape about names. She's more than my grandma. It's like she's my mother, even though she isn't and even if she is as old as Methuselah.

Mamina's got a couple of kids of her own. The older son's been in jail for twenty years, the younger one has been in the wind for the past fifteen. He works in a cement plant in Patagonia. Silvio, I think his name is. I don't know what he looks like, I've never met him. Actually, I might have seen him once when I was a kid but I don't remember.

Anyway, it's only because of this Silvio that I didn't end up out on the street – me and the other kids Mamina got lumbered with. When we got dumped on her, Mamina was too old to go out cleaning people's houses. But ever since he fucked off, her son Silvio sends money every month. It's not much, but it's enough to keep Mamina alive. And not just her. The feckless kids she looked after are gone now, pissed off a couple of years ago. I'm the only one left and Mamina knows I'll be moving on too any day now. But I stick around because I'd feel bad leaving her on her own.

'Where did you get this?' Mamina asks, not taking her hand out of the pocket of her apron.

'Nowhere . . . I've been doing odd jobs.'

'That's what I like to hear, *m'hijo.*' She stops me short. She's not buying it. She doesn't like it when I lie to her. And I don't like lying to her either, but I've got no choice.

Mamina waves for me to go. And I go.

BURNING A HOLE

I pay for my ticket like a proper gentleman and board the train. Life's easier when you've got money. And it's better too: the sky is bluer, the heat is more bearable, even the passengers I'm sharing the carriage with seem like decent people. But I still can't shake off the shreds of fear clinging to me. Anyway, I haven't a fucking clue where I want to go or what I want to do. I've spent years dreaming of having the cash to be able to do the things I want, but now I've got it, I don't know what they are. 'I don't know what the fuck I want,' I mutter, thinking about skinhead Lucas, 'but I want it now.' At least I know that much.

I count the money discreetly, so as not to get dirty looks from the passengers. It's not exactly a fortune, but it's enough to finance my vices for a couple of months. Or I could blow the lot in a couple of days.

In Buenos Aires, I get off the train at Belgrano station and walk down Entre Ríos towards the centre. It's a bit of a slog, but the whole city's gridlocked. There's marches and demos and picketers everywhere – striking teachers, old-age pensioners, the unemployed, civil servants, everyone's out demonstrating against something. Police cars and sirens. But as I cross the Plaza Congreso there's not a living soul. Callao, Corrientes and the Avenida de Mayo have been cordoned off by the *milicos* – the cops. At Talcahuano I run into a little group of students with flags, placards, signs, whistles and rattles marching under a huge banner. They're taking orders from some skinny guy in glasses who's shouting into a megaphone. There's only four of them, but they're acting like there's a crowd stretching all the way back to Liniers. What's really fucking funny is they haven't sussed they're heading straight for the police cordon about two hundred metres up ahead.

I stand for a minute, amazed, watching them pass – particularly this one girl in a Rasta cap who's so fucking hot it's a crime, marching with a sexy little swing of her hips. Half a block from the cordon, she stops dancing and the kids sit down in the middle of the street to weigh up the situation. It's all bullshit, an act.

I leave them there and head down Lavalle. I go into the first cinema I find open and buy a ticket without even asking what's on. The cashier hands me back way too much change.

'First screening is half price,' she says seeing my surprise.

Inside the cinema, I can only make out three people in the semi-darkness. It's some Yank movie. A shoot-'em-up. Five minutes in I'm already bored rigid, but I stay to the end. And it ends just like I expect. Happy ever after. Piece of shit.

I go out, spark up a *negro* and wander about for a bit. I'm hungry. I go into a pizza place and order the most expensive pizza on the menu – it's got everything: mushrooms, ham, artichokes, peppers . . .

'Thick crust, chief,' I say to the waiter, indicating the thickness with my thumb and index finger. 'And a beer . . .' I pick the most expensive beer too. It's imported. Black as Coca-Cola. And it's lush.

I stuff myself till I'm full. I almost can't finish, but I force myself. When I go to pay, it's the cinema ticket all over again.

'Today's offer is the house special and a beer,' the waiter explains.

I pay up and leave. I walk around aimlessly and, without meaning to, I find myself in the Once district. I haven't been here for years. The old Jewish businesses are still here, but not the Jews. It's all Koreans now. I only see one Jewish family walking hand in hand down the street in their Sunday best – the mother and the two daughters in long skirts, the father in black with a broad-brimmed hat and those two long curls that hang down from the sideburns. The little boy is wearing short trousers and a tiny hat, a sort of skullcap held on with hairpins like the ones Mamina uses.

On the opposite pavement, two Peruvians are arguing over a whore. A chubby girl, pretty enough. I'm not really paying them any attention. Neither are the Jewish family. They keep walking. The argument gets louder and eventually the two guys come to blows. The short fat one headbutts the other guy and breaks his nose. Looks to me like we have a winner. Show's over. But the crowd of gawpers doesn't move. They're waiting to see how it turns out. I leave them to it.

I stop in front of a shoe-shop window and see the pair of shoes I've been wanting for ages. I go in. I'm all happy when it turns out they're the most expensive pair in the shop. It's stupid, but to me it's funny. I try them on, but when I check them out in the mirror, they look too flash. I wouldn't make it to the next street corner wearing these – with the country fucked up the way it is, it's just asking to be mugged. I find something more low-profile, but when it comes to paying for them, it's the same shit again. Turns out they're on special offer. I tell the girl in the shop not to bother wrapping them, I'll wear them. I leave my old pair with her. They're no use to anyone.

They're got rips on both sides and the soles have split.

I head down towards the port. The afternoon is drawing in and I still can't seem to shake off the fear. I've got money burning a hole in my pocket, but with all the fucking special offers and half-price promotions, I can't manage to get rid of it. Probably for the best, I tell myself, but I'm not really convinced.

Passing a bookshop I go in and browse around. I'm prepared to buy pretty much anything by this stage. Among the dusty, dog-eared books, there's one that catches my eye. A fat book with a drawing of a white whale ripping apart a ship full of sailors on the cover. *Moby Dick*, it's called. I like the drawing, I don't really know why. I look at it for a bit, then I remember this cartoon with a flying whale I used to watch when I was a kid. It was a bit gay but I liked it. I used to watch it on the colour TV cousin Toni brought round one day. Probably robbed it.

The whale on the cover is just like the one on TV. Same shape, same eyes, but it looks more savage, more realistic. It's a proper whale.

I space out, thinking about cousin Toni. He was my hero back when I was a kid. He smoked, he dated girls and he always used to give me money. I must have been about ten at the time. And it's been ten years since I last saw him. He disappeared. He got himself mixed up in some shit. They say he was on the Feds' most wanted list.

'I'll take this,' I say to the old guy dozing behind a pile of books.

He gets up, stretches, takes the book I'm holding.

'This one's really good, it's a classic!' he tells me. 'That'll be four pesos.'

Fuck knows what I think I'm doing. I've read exactly one book in my whole life, and here I am buying another one. To make matters worse, the guy's practically giving it away when all I was trying to do was get rid of my money . . .

PEACE AND LOVE

I walk down towards the port, book tucked under my arm, hands in my pockets. In the right-hand pocket I feel Yanina's spliff. I didn't want to smoke it earlier because I was feeling a bit freaked out and when I smoke weed it always heightens whatever I'm feeling. If I'm bummed, it messes me up. If I'm happy, it makes me ecstatic. If I'm freaked out, it makes me completely fucking paranoid.

But now I feel maybe I might spark it up. The whale cheered me up – not the one on the cover of the book, the one on TV. It was huge but it could shrink down to the size of a drop of water. Josefina, it was called. I even remember the theme song. When it got bigger again, it would fly off with a little boy on its back. Somewhere far away. It was cool. I don't know why I'm still thinking about cousin Toni. He kind of reminds me of the kid in the cartoon. Maybe when I was little, when Toni disappeared, I dreamed he flew away on the back of the whale.

I zigzag across the fourteen lanes of the Avenida 9 de Julio, brakes screeching, horns honking. I'm completely out of it and I haven't even sparked up the spliff yet. I cut into the park looking for a quiet place for a toke. There's not many people around. One or two couples sitting under the trees, a few kids playing football. On the steps around the fountain are some people selling crafts, with all their stuff on blankets in front of them. I amble towards them, then suddenly I freeze. I start trembling. I can't fucking believe it. I rub my eyes hard and look again, but it's definitely him. His hair is longer and he's got a bit of a beard going, but it's definitely him. He's twisting a piece of wire and chatting to some long-haired guy. He hasn't seen me. I light a cigarette, trying to calm down. This can't be an accident. It's too much of a coincidence.

I psych myself up and walk over to stand in front of the stuff he's got laid out on his blanket, like I'm thinking of buying something. He doesn't look up. He goes on doing what he's doing. I kick the carved hash pipe nearest me so it rolls towards him forcing him to finally react.

'What the fuck d'you think you're doing?' he yells, looking up and staring me hard in the eye. It takes a couple of seconds before he recognises me and jumps up.

'*Gringuito!* Fucking hell!' he yells into my ear, lifting me off the ground with a bear hug.

'Toni . . . Jesus fucking . . .' I can't finish the sentence because I've got a lump in my throat the size of a grapefruit.

Any minute now, I'm going to start bawling and I don't want him to think I'm some punk bitch. We keep hugging and kissing until the feeling passes.

'I thought the fuckers had killed you . . .' I say, squeezing his arm. I still can't believe it.

'In their dreams.'

'Couple of years later, I ran into this guy who told me you'd fucked off to Brazil.'

'Yeah, I was there for a bit,' he says with a cheeky smile, '*mas agora eu fico aqui, maluco*.'

'Huh . . . ?' I've no fucking clue what he just said. Toni bursts out laughing. So do I.

'It means now I'm back, *loco*.'

'Yeah, so far back you've turned into a filthy hippy,' I bait him.

'What do you want? It's tough on the streets, *viejo*.' He laughs again, but then says seriously, 'It's a jungle out here, *loco*, I'm not shitting you. And I'm tired of living in fear. There comes a point when you just want to slam the door and move somewhere else, but you can't get out. And no matter how bad things are, they can always get worse. You know why?'

He pauses like this is a riddle. I look at him quizzically.

'Because the jungle's inside you, *loco*. There is no outside, there's nowhere to go.'

'Wow! That's deep . . .' I say, breaking the awkward silence. 'Don't tell me you're a Jehovah's Witness now?'

Toni shits himself laughing.

'Love and peace, brother.' He makes the V-sign, still laughing his arse off. When he's done laughing, he claps me on the back, hugs me again, pinches my cheek.

'It's good to see you, Gringuito. Fuck but you've grown . . .'

He's right. When I was a kid Toni looked like a giant to me. These days, I'm half a head taller than him.

'But hey, tell me, what are you doing here? Were you on the march?'

'Like I give a shit . . .'

'Where's your solidarity, comrade?!' he says, raising his fist in a salute. Now it's his turn to take the piss.

But it turns out that it's only because of the march that we ran into each other. The artisans' union were on the march. They're not affiliated but they came to show solidarity, Toni explains, introducing me to his friends. El Piti, a scrawny guy, his face thin like a smack addict, scarred and pockmarked; then there's Laurita, a girl with big tits and her face painted green.

They never come into Buenos Aires. The Feds are always hassling them about street vendors' permits, so with what they make it isn't worth the hassle. It's not even enough to bribe the cops to turn a blind eye. They prefer to hang out in the Tigre Delta, he says, because most of the year it's a stop-off for foreign tourists. Gullible tourists prepared to splash out wads of cash on 'genuine native artefacts'. Actually, the beads they use in the necklaces come from China and the alloy wire is mined in Africa.

'But come on, Gringo, spill, what's going on? How's Mamina? What's been happening in the barrio?'

Same old, same old. What can I tell him . . . ? I make an effort, try to make it sound more interesting than it is, but I just can't do it. It's hardly surprising. There's nothing to say. But he keeps asking about Mamina, so I tell him, 'She's getting on a bit now . . . Why don't you drop by and see her sometime? She'd be stoked . . .'

'I can't, Gringo. I've got unfinished business in the barrio. Probably best I don't show my face there.' He looks at me seriously. 'But give her a big kiss from me and tell her I think about her all the time.'

Another awkward silence falls on us, the air so thick you could run a comb through it. And now's not a good time to make jokes.

'Hang on there a second, I'll be right back,' I say.

I throw the book I've still got under my arm

onto his mat and dash off. A couple of minutes later I'm back with five bottles of beer. Two in each hand and one under my arm. The tribe give me a round of applause. Using lighters, pliers, teeth, they've popped the caps in half a second and the beers are doing the rounds.

'A spliff in your honour, you filthy hippy!' I say to Toni, finally sparking Yanina's joint.

It was worth hanging on to it. I see him smiling through the smoke. I take a couple of tokes and pass it. He does the same, holding the smoke in. He nods at the book, laughs, coughs, chokes . . .

'I see you're an intellectual these days, Gringo,' he says mockingly.

'Too right!' I say, putting on a posh, scholarly face.

'Hey, Piti,' he nudges his friend, jerking his thumb at the book, 'Gringo here is reading one of your favourites . . .'

'*Uy!* It's the whale,' says Piti laughing to himself. 'Got to be very careful when you're dealing with the whale, *loco*.'

I tell him I haven't even started reading it yet so I've no idea what he's on about. But all I get from him is the same warning. He's being all mysterious.

'You'll see . . .' he says.

We go on drinking and chatting and joking. They're good people. I feel at home with them. Toni reels off stories about his travels and about his time living on the streets. Some of the stories sound kind of sketchy, but I believe them anyway. Then he gets to talking about some bad memories of the barrio. And he does it because he realises I know what he's talking about, I can put myself in his shoes, I understand him perfectly. Even the spaces between the words.

It's pitch dark by now. There's no one left in the park and the hawkers are starting to pack up and leave. I've been slyly winkling info out of Toni about his work, trying to get as much as I can. It's got its ups and downs, but there's money to be made year-round. Not much, but enough to get by. The secret is to keep moving, not to stay in one place for more than two or three months. Toni's group hangs out in the Delta. They head down to the Atlantic coast from time to time, or up into the hills, to Córdoba. When it gets too hot, they head south and do the Lake District around Bariloche.

'So, is it hard work?' I'm not beating about the bush any more.

'Nah . . . With a bit of patience and someone to show you a couple of things, you're set. The rest you learn as you go.'

'So what would you need to start?' I ask straight out. He knows what I'm getting at.

'Don't tell me you want to take up a trade?'

'Thinking about it,' I tell him. And it's true.

'Well, depends on what you want to make . . .'

'What do I know? Necklaces, earrings, bracelets
. . . All the shit you make.'

Toni gets excited now and starts trying to
explain everything. If you're going to make a living,
the important thing is to work in groups. Keep
things moving, make stuff that's seasonal.
Concentrate on jewellery around Christmas and
when you're in the mountains. In summer, churn
out the threads and braids girls like to put in their
hair. At the beach, there's big money to be made
doing henna tattoos. During school term, the best
thing to make is hash pipes, because kids are
always into paraphernalia.

He's about to tell me some more, but he can tell
from my expression that I need him to be more
specific. He starts bundling his stuff into his blanket
and goes back to talking about jewellery. He talks
about alpaca, tin, silver; plate and alloy wire – length
in metres, diameter in millimetres – about semi-
precious stones, paste jewellery, beads, glass. I'm
completely confused, and I'm getting annoyed now.

'Yeah, but how much to get started?'

He starts calculating, pulling numbers out of
the air.

'Just a rough guess, Toni.'

He gives me a figure. I do a quick calculation of
what I've got left in my pocket after my spending
spree, and figure I've got more than enough.

'Then there's the tools. To start off, you'll need a

couple of pairs of needle-nose pliers, nail clippers, a jeweller's hammer. But don't worry, I can front you for a while.'

'OK, Toni, that's enough to be going on with, *viejo*.' With everything he's told me, I'm already excited.

We say nothing for a couple of minutes but when he's finished packing up he says, 'When you make up your mind, let me know. I've got this girl I work with who'll do me a good price, she'll even bankroll me.'

'How do I find you?'

'We're out on an island in the Tigre Delta until next month.' He takes a scrap of paper and a biro from his backpack and writes out the address. 'It's easy to find. You can't miss it,' he says looking at me and smiling. 'But I'll give you the girl's phone number. Cristina, her name is; she always knows where to find us.'

I slip the piece of paper into my book and say goodbye. Toni doesn't say anything. He gives me a big hug and slopes off with the rest of the gang. After a couple of steps he turns and gives me a wink. And I stand there, alone in the park, sorting things out in my head.

HEADING BACK

There's fifteen minutes before the train leaves. It's the last one back to the barrio. I check the time on the rusty panel in Buenos Aires station. A guard has just turned the handle that controls the three timetables: destinations, times, platforms. After mine, on the south branch line, there's one train twenty minutes later heading south-west. After that, nothing.

If I'd hung around a little longer, I'd have had to spend the night in the station. And I can't say I much fancy the idea. There's not even a clean bench you could stretch out on. Next to the ticket office a filthy tramp is setting up cardboard boxes to bed down for the night. Further along, a cripple with a begging sign is ranting and raving like some psycho. He's necking a carton of panther piss and arguing with the ghosts clouding his vision. To complete the set, a dark-skinned guy with a pockmarked face is closing up the news-stand and kicking the metal shutter down.

Up on the platforms there's a gang of kids sniffing glue from Coke cans. Not much chance of a good night's sleep with them around. When they're stoned, they could easily set fire to you while you're asleep – just for a laugh. I think I recognise one of them from the barrio. I think he hangs with Quique, but I'm not sure. They're all the same, those kids. Doesn't matter whether they've got mothers, fathers, brothers, their real family is on the street. Chueco was like that. So was I. But we're grown up now and we've got things sussed. No one calls us sons of the street now, they call us sons of bitches.

I dodge a couple of delinquents fucking around on the platform and spot a café that's still open. I go in and sit at the counter. The guy's already closing up. He's just finished cleaning the coffee machine and started in on the grill. He picks out a piece of dried-up meat and puts it on a plate. Just as he's about to throw away a burnt piece of sausage, I say, 'Hey, if you're going to toss it, give it to me, boss.'

The guy turns and glares at me. He obviously doesn't find the joke funny. I back down, I don't want any grief.

'Could I get a sausage sandwich, please boss, and a glass of wine?'

'If you want it hot, you got no chance, kid, there's no charcoal on the grill.'

'No, as it comes is fine . . .' I say.

While he's dealing with the food, I fumble for my money. A handful of coins to pay him. I slip the number Toni gave me and a couple of big bills into my book. I put the rest back into my pocket. The wine is even worse than the muck Fat Farías sells and the bread is stale. When you're served rat poison there's nothing you can do. I use the bread to sop up the *chimichurri* sauce which makes it just about edible. As I'm taking the second bite, I hear my train called over the loudspeaker. I knock back the wine, pay up and leave, still chewing.

By the time I climb aboard the train, it's already pulling out. I walk through the carriages towards the front of the train. I don't really know why – it's not like there's no empty seats. There are only a couple of passengers in each carriage, stretched out so they can sleep. In the third carriage, I see her. She's sitting in a window seat, her back to me. I recognise her straight off. Without thinking, I plonk myself down next to her.

'Yani! *Qué onda?*'

'Fine,' she says, startled. 'How are things with you?' She's lying; she looks terrible. It's hardly surprising.

'How's your old man?' I ask. I sound like an arsehole, but I genuinely want to know.

'You heard then? He's OK. I'm just on my way back from the hospital. The doctors did X-rays and a brain scan, and it turns out there's no serious damage, thank God. They gave him five stitches, put a dressing on the gash in his head. He's got a broken rib, but it's not serious. They're letting him out tomorrow.'

'That's good. Are you going to pick him up?'

'No. El Jetita is going to collect him in his car,' she says.

'El Jetita?' I slip up.

'Yeah. It's really weird,' she says, studying me carefully. 'These days, he and my old man are inseparable as arsecrack and underpants. He even showed up at the hospital today . . .'

I swallow hard, trying to think of a way out of this mess.

'What about you? How are you bearing up?'

'Fine . . .'

'What's with the face then? Were you worried?'

'No, of course not. I knew he'd be fine. You know what my old man's like. By the time I found him, he was washing the blood out of his hair, and was all for closing up the wound with superglue. Didn't even want to see a doctor. It took me an age to get him to go to the first-aid clinic.'

'So what is it then? What's up with you?'

She clicks her tongue, sighs, stares out the window. She's pissed off or she's scared, one of the two. But mostly, she's cute. Her mouth tightens up like a purple flower. She half closes her eyes and the ends of her eyebrows curve upward. She looks like a cat on heat. All she needs is a pair of little pointy ears. She pushes back her long black hair and gives me a sidelong glance.

'OK, I'll tell you, Gringo, but you can't say a word to anyone, OK?' She's staring at me evenly now.

I try to read her eyes, but they're inscrutable. I nod and wait for her to say something.

'I'm worried about what's going on between El Jetita and my old man. I don't know what deal they've got going, but whatever it is I don't like it. El Jetita's following me around all the time and coming on to me and *papá* doesn't say anything . . .'

'Because your Papá is a first-class cunt,' I think, and the more I think about it the angrier I get. Fat Farías has always been the gamekeeper, keeping poachers away from his little girl, and now he's prepared to serve her up on a plate to that fucking pervert. Either he's getting something out of the deal – and it would have to be something big, otherwise it wouldn't make sense – or else El Jetita's got him by the balls and he's got no choice but to turn a blind eye. But whatever the reason, the fat fucker is prepared to peddle his own daughter. I should have let Chueco kick him all the way into the next barrio.

'Don't let it get to you, Yani,' I say, choking back my anger. 'You can count on me, anything you need . . .'

She looks at me sceptically. I go on.

'El Jetita's a fucking psycho, playing the gangster. Someone needs to put a stop to it, that's all.'

'And you're the one to stop it?' she asks mischievously and smiles at me.

'What, you think I'm chicken?' I say like it's a joke, but I'm deadly serious.

Yani does her best to change the subject and I go along with it for the next couple of stops, but after that we sit in silence. Each deep in our thoughts.

A conductor comes through the carriages closing the metal blinds. He nods for Yani to pull down the one next to her. He doesn't bother to explain – not that he needs to, we know the deal – and goes on his way. We're coming into prime stone-throwing territory – kids throwing rocks big enough to split the head of anyone dumb enough to have the windows open in summer, or smash the train window in winter. I've seen it happen. But it's all quiet this trip. Nothing going bump in the night.

Yani tries to pick up the conversation, asks what I've been up to. I lie a bit, and then tell her what I did with my day. She asks about the book, and I lie again, try to sound interesting. She talks about the books her teacher had her read for class last year. *El Matadero*, which was disgusting, and *Amalia*, which she loved. This year she's doing her final exams.

'Are you going to keep it up? The studying?'

'Don't know. What about you?'

'What about me?' I glare at her.

She looks embarrassed and I regret the words straight away. I make like a mental defective, ask her to repeat the question and she laughs and we're cool again.

'I was only asking if you're planning on finishing school, babes. They run a class at night school for adults to take their exams. You're nineteen, right, you're an adult? Three years and you could have a qualification.'

'I don't know. Maybe if I could get a cushy morning job I might go back to school.'

The train is pulling in. The station is dark. I say the first thing that comes into my head, trying to sound mysterious and enigmatic to make her laugh. And she does. I love the way her cheeks dimple when she smiles. She's so pretty. Just hearing her laugh turns me on. I imagine her laughing like that, stark naked. For me, in my bed.

We stand there for a minute or two until the train pulls out. We're about to say goodbye. I'm going across the tracks, she'll be heading down the hill. I tell her again, seriously this time, that if she has any trouble with El Jetita she can count on me. She thanks me. She kisses me on the cheek like we've been friends our whole lives, and then she's gone.

INVESTMENTS

There's been no sign of Quique today which is weird, given that it's Saturday. And Mamina hasn't said a word to me. We had lunch in silence, some sort of stew with a few noodles, a couple of cabbage leaves and stray scraps of meat floating in it. I'm guessing it cost most of the money I gave her yesterday. But I don't dare ask. I just eat. When Mamina isn't talking it's because she's got nothing good to say. And since it's not like she's afraid to say what she thinks, it's better not to provoke her. Right now she's having a siesta.

I'm reading the whale book in the little courtyard out the back. I didn't go out this morning, didn't feel like it. Don't feel like it now but I'm tired of prowling round the house like an animal in a cage. A very small cage. I spend the afternoon drinking *mate* and listening to last night's stock-car race at Turismo Carretera until I get bored.

I'm reading to take my mind off things, but I still feel panicky. Ishmael, the guy telling the story, is a cook and whenever he gets panicky and feels like putting a bullet in his brain, he boards a ship and sets off somewhere. Doesn't care where he's headed, he says, but this time it looks like he's got a good idea because he holes up overnight in this strange little inn and waits a day and a half for a boat that goes to an island from where the whaling ships set sail.

The way he talks is kind of weird, but I know exactly how he's feeling. Makes me feel I should do the same thing. Probably wouldn't be that easy. I've never tried stowing aboard a cargo ship down at the port, but if I did, I'm sure I'd be chucked overboard. Or they'd take me for a thief and throw me in jail.

I keep reading, but I can't concentrate. I'm not getting anywhere. It's the middle of the afternoon and the sun seems to be setting already. The stubby fig tree in the courtyard is starting to block the weak, orangey light. Every now and then the wind turns the page before I'm done reading it, and I have to turn back. The breeze is chilly. Autumn's coming in.

I feel someone watching me. I look up and I see Chueco looking over the courtyard wall.

'What the fuck are you doing, gay boy? Since when did you start reading books?'

I don't answer. I settle myself on the plastic crate, lean back against the wall, pretend to keep reading. Chueco throws a leg over the wall, jumps down and comes towards me. He stops about three feet away and stands there, legs apart, blocking the light.

'Don't tell me you're blowing the money I gave you on this shit, kid. Me, I invested my share of the take,' he says, opening his denim jacket so I can see the fucker's strapped.

'Can I have a look?' I reach out.

As he tries to take the gun out of his belt, he gets the trigger guard caught in his T-shirt and starts swearing and tugging. For all his gangster posing, he obviously hasn't a fucking clue. He holds it out to me, but instead of twirling it on his finger and offering me the butt, he points it at me.

'Fuck sake, Chueco, what the hell are you doing?!' I shout, flinching.

I shouldn't have shouted, I should have smashed his face in. It's loaded. It's a .38. It looks cool, a bit battered but recently blued. The original butt must have broken off at some point because it's got a new pale wood butt held together with rivets with the heads sanded down, but it looks hard.

'Where did you get it?' I ask, handing the gun back.

'What the fuck you care?' he snaps.

He laughs, puts on his best thug face and starts

waving the thing around. Chueco is off his head. The fucker's more dangerous than a monkey with a machete, I'm thinking, trying to stay out of the line of fire – which is hard since he's spinning his arm like a windmill.

'So, what, you figure you've got a career as a gangster?' I say, but he's not listening. He's acting his part, all he needs is a film crew. He makes like he's pulling the gun from an armpit holster and threatening some invisible guy. He pokes it into the guy's kidneys, the barrel pressed right against his body, grabbing him by the throat with his left hand. He plays the scene out, pretends to fire, making *bang, bang* noises like a kid, firing all over the place, steadying the gun with his left hand. He fires up, fires down, spins round and goes on capping a bunch of ghosts. He finishes by stretching his arm out and trying to turn the gun on himself. When he's finally tired of play-acting, he says, 'If the señorita is done with her books and wants to try out my new work tool, I've got no problem with that.'

I don't think twice.

'Let's go,' I say.

We get to the patch of waste ground that used to be a football pitch and is now a rubbish tip and Chueco picks up a one-litre can. A bit dented but intact. He positions it on a clear patch of ground and backs off five metres. He aims, fires and misses. By a mile. It raises a spray of dirt about a foot and a half from the can.

'Let's see what the señorita can do,' he says and passes me the gun.

'Keep it up with that shit and I'll split your head open,' I say.

'Bring it on, señorita . . .'

'Don't say I didn't warn you,' I say, taking aim.

Chueco always did know how to wind me up. I don't know how he manages it, but he always does. Weird, because when it's some random fuckwit trying to wind me up, I don't give a shit.

Just as I'm about to squeeze the trigger he nudges me to make me miss. And I miss, but not by much. I aim again, holding my breath.

'What are you doing?' he yells.

I ignore him and concentrate. I remember what Toni used to tell me when I was a kid about how to fire a gun. He'd take me down to the patch of waste ground that used to be on the other side of the stream before they fenced it off to make a golf course and build a gated community. Toni always managed to bag a partridge, sometimes a hare. They say the place is teeming with animals these days. And it's not hard to believe – even without going inside the gate it's obvious the golf course is nothing but scrubland. But no one goes in there any more, and with all the security guards watching the perimeter they sure as fuck wouldn't go strapped.

It's like riding a bike, you never forget, I tell myself, spreading my legs to distribute my weight, right foot forward like Toni taught me, tracing an invisible line between the eye, the sight and the target. It was easier with Toni's shotgun, even if it did weigh a ton, because it was like a ruler – all you had to do was line it up, hold your breath and gently squeeze the trigger. If your aim was a bit off, the spread of shotgun pellets helped. Obviously if the partridge was on the wing, it was harder because then you had to trace a moving invisible line, but anything on the ground was easy. I got sick of shooting rats and weasels. I even managed to do pretty well with the .22 Toni used to have. The only difference was you had to stretch your arm out and use that as your ruler. Oh, and the recoil didn't fuck your shoulder up. With the .22, the recoil was just a quick jolt, but Toni's shotgun had a serious kickback to it. If you didn't brace it properly, you'd end up with bruises on your shoulder.

Chueco's talking to me, but I'm not listening. I hold my breath and I fire. The can whips up into the air and falls back almost in the same place, now presenting the full moon of its base. I raise the .38 and fire again. The can shudders again.

'What the fuck are you doing, dickwad?' Chueco says, snatching the gun from me. 'D'you know how much bullets cost?'

He fires a couple more shots, misses, keeps
firing until the chamber's empty. He takes a box of
bullets from his jacket pocket and reloads. He goes
on shooting, not bothering to pass it to me any
more, until he finally hits the can.

'Who would have thought little Gringo could
handle himself with a gat . . . ?' he says like he's
talking to someone else.

There's not a trace of the gangster face he had
on a while ago. Now he's looking at me strangely.
Seriously. Part defiant, part devious as he stuffs the
gun back in his belt. God knows what's going
through his head.

'Why don't you get yourself a bit of kit like this
one? Then you can be my sidekick,' he suggests.
'I've already got a couple of bits of business lined
up. You want in, fine, if not, don't come whining to
me when I'm rich and fat.'

'So what's this "business", Chueco?'

'Come by El Gordo's later and I'll fill you in.'

'Farías's place? Are you off your head?'

'What's the matter? Chicken?' he taunts me.
Here we go again.

'Fuck you, you fucking jerk! You go ahead. You
do your shady little deals and you'll wind up with
your arse facing north.'

I storm off, giving him the finger as I leave. I
feel calm, but I know me. I know sooner or later
I'll swing by the bar.

MAGGOT OF A DOUBT

'You'll never guess who I ran into in Buenos Aires yesterday . . .' I say to Mamina, as she sips the sweet *mate* I've just brewed for her.

I wait for her to ask who, but nothing. She doesn't even look at me.

'Someone who was asking after you, *abuela*. Don't you want to know who it was?'

'Who?'

'Toni!'

Mamina doesn't react. Or she does, but in her own way. She stares out the window. For what feels like a century. She empties the rest of the sachet of sugar into her *mate* and adds some more hot water. She takes a sip, then looks at me. I've seen this look before, cold as hoar frost, but I don't understand it. I've never been able to understand it. And I certainly don't now. I open my eyes wide, raise my eyebrows, feeling a wave of panic grip me. I'm waiting for her to explain. Mamina knows that.

She's not stupid. She calmly finishes her *mate* and then says abruptly, 'Toni is dead.'

'What do you mean, dead?' I explode. 'I just said I saw him, that he said to say hi . . . What are you talking about?'

Mamina answers, her voice low. Almost inaudible. She always hates it when people raise their voices. When they do, she starts whispering. I used to think it was funny when I was a kid. I'd do it deliberately to wind her up. The softer she spoke, the louder I shouted. Never worked. Mamina always won. Didn't matter how violent the argument, we always ended up whispering.

'He's dead to me. He doesn't exist . . . And I don't want to discuss it any further.'

'What's up, Mamina? What did he do?'

'You don't know?'

'Obviously not, since I'm asking you . . .' I retort, but I'm careful not to raise my voice above her whisper.

'Good, that's good. It's better if you don't know . . .'

I clear away the *mate*. There's no point carrying on. When Mamina decides a subject is closed, there's no arguing. It's closed, full stop, end of story.

I go back and sit at the kitchen table. I rack my brains but I can't remember anything. I was only a kid. I would have been – what? – ten, maybe, when Toni disappeared. Not even. Whatever shit he got himself mixed up in must have been serious. Really fucking serious, if Mamina still hasn't forgiven him. She's not the kind to hold a grudge.

All this just makes me suspicious, tarnishes the image I've had of Toni. Makes me see him differently. Like he's a traitor, a son of a bitch. Toni said he couldn't come back to the barrio because he had 'unfinished business'. I'm guessing this unfinished business is the same thing Mamina refuses to talk about. I used to think Toni disappeared because the Feds were looking for him, but that's bullshit. Nobody leaves the barrio just because the cops are after them. Nobody gives a shit about the police round here; the only law is the law of the barrio, and most kids are careful to abide by it. Anyone who doesn't would do well to fuck off before they get sent to a barrio six feet under. That must be what happened with Toni, but I can't think what shit he could have got himself mixed up in that meant having to vanish without trace. And is whatever it is the same shit that Mamina can't forgive him for?

I can't seem to square the two. For Toni to disappear like that means a vendetta, a *mejicaneada*, score-settling for some scam that went wrong – but all those things are about honour, about the code of the barrio. And

Mamina's not the kind to turn her back on one of her own for something like that. She has her own personal code, and it's very different. So, what then? She can't forgive him for abandoning her, leaving her in the lurch and not showing his face for years? I can't believe that either. It's not like her. It's a luxury she can't afford. The luxury of a middle-class mother more interested in her own pain than the fate of her ungrateful child.

Too many questions. I hate people asking me questions. I hate it even more when it's me doing the asking and I don't have any answers. I lie on my bed and try to take my mind off things by reading the whale book, but I can't focus. I keep turning it all over and over in my mind. I keep turning the book over and over, until the money and the scrap of paper with Toni's address fall out. I count the money again, and read the note again: they're my ticket out of here, but now I'm not sure I want to leave. At least not until I find out what the fuck went down between Toni and Mamina.

The sun's sinking. There's not much light left. It's too early to head over to Farías's bar, but I've nowhere else to go. I'm drowning here.

'I'm heading out, Mamina,' I tell her. 'I won't be back for dinner.'

She answers with a wave, flicking the back of her hand without even looking at me.

Instead of taking the alley up towards the

station, I wander along one of the dirt tracks leading off it. The one that runs past the house of Oliviera, the Portuguese guy. This way, I have to take the bridge across the train tracks. It's the long way round. I'm killing time.

It's pretty quiet for a Saturday. There's almost no sound from the row of shacks. I can hear muffled music from one of them, a burst of laughter from another, but nothing else. The buildings round here aren't so much bricks and mortar as corrugated iron and bits of timber. In the evening light, they look derelict.

Two little kids are throwing stones at a mangy, pitiful dog. The dog shambles away – hasn't got the energy to run. Not that he needs to, given the kids' aim. They couldn't hit a cow at ten feet. They're only snotty-nosed little tykes with no shoes.

At the end of the lane, just before the tracks, I turn and, after about thirty metres, find myself in front of Ernestina's place. Without even thinking, I've come to fetch Quique. I've obviously got used to having the kid around. When he's not, I kind of miss him.

I cup my hands like an ocarina, put my lips to my thumbs and whistle, the call of a non-existent bird. Quique knows it. He's been trying to get the hang of it for months but either he's got his hands clasped wrong, or he's not blowing at the right angle. He keeps asking me to tell him how to do it, but I don't know how to explain. So I show him again, but instead of watching, he closes his eyes and listens, like if he can just get the sound right, the rest will come by itself.

I give another bird call and Sultán barks at me. He's tied up round the back. Quique doesn't show. He can't not have heard me. I blow hard. I pop my head over the bamboo fence. No one about. The door is padlocked. His kid sister's doll is lying in the yard, wearing the fur from the cat that me and Chueco ate the other day. I laugh because the pelt looks like it was made-to-measure. It's turned right side out now – with the fur on the outside – and wearing it, the doll looks like some crazy old woman with a shock of hair and a mink coat showing off her legs.

I push the chain-link gate, go into the yard and pick up the doll, laughing to myself. The old woman turns out to be a bit skanky. And she stinks. The arms of her fur coat have claws on the end ready to scratch someone's eyes out. The cat obviously bared its claws before it died and they stayed like that, stiff and razor-sharp. I stare at one of the claws and it's moving. It's nearly night, so I can't really see properly. I hold the doll up to my face, gagging on the putrid stench, and I see the claw isn't a claw. It's wriggling like it's waving to me. It's a maggot, a two-day-old fly larva. I've seen enough flyblown animals that I don't need to strip the doll to know its teeming with maggots. That's one sight I'd rather spare myself. I open my hands and the plastic body bounces on the ground. If the old woman were flesh and blood, they'd be eating her alive.

OLD DEBTS

Fat Farías looks like a sultan. He's got a white turban of bandages round his head, he's wearing his shirt open and he's got bruises all the way down to his man boobs. His left arm is bandaged too. He's using some filthy, snotty handkerchief as a sling. He's sitting at a table like a lord. Serious. Talking to Rubén.

The bar is practically empty. The drunks in the barrio are loyal as cats. Farías only has to close up for one day and they've already found some other dive. It'll be a while before they're back. I see Chueco sitting in the far corner, staring into his glass. El Jetita is standing beside him, leaning down, hand on Chueco's shoulder, whispering something in his ear, looking like an old friend, like a big brother giving his kid brother advice. What the fuck is going on here?

'Hey, Gringo!' Chueco calls over to me. 'Over here! Pull up a chair!'

I'm threading my way between the tables when I

see her, standing behind the bar where her father should be, pouring a glass of red wine for some old guy. She puts the cork back in the bottle and looks up. She's beautiful. She's got her hair pinned up and she's wearing a dark apron. The thin shoulder straps emphasise her long, bare, slender neck. I feel like covering her in kisses. But Yani's staring at me like she doesn't recognise me. Makes sense, I suppose. After all, in here I'm a customer and she's staff. Though, come to think of it, I'm not sure I've ever seen her working behind her old man's bar before. I've seen her come in and ask him for money or chat to him, but I've never seen her serving.

I'm staring so hard I walk slap bang into the back of a chair and nearly rupture my balls. I swear under my breath. Yani tries not to laugh, but she carries on wiping down the counter, she doesn't look over. When she finally lifts her head, I shoot her a look of sheer agony that makes her laugh out loud. I love the way her cheeks dimple. Her laugh makes us partners in crime just like it did last night. When she finally stops giggling, I give her an enquiring look, jerk my chin, raise my eyebrows. She frowns, glancing quickly in three different directions – the table where Fat Farías is chatting with Rubén, the table at the back where Chueco and El Jetita are huddled, and the old man at the bar she's just been serving. El Negro Sosa is propping up the bar. I hadn't noticed him. That means the whole gang is here. There's some shit going down, and if someone doesn't tell me what the fuck is going on and soon, I'm gone. I'll be out of here before the tango starts, because I know my luck: I always wind up with the ugly best friend. If I have to tango, I'd rather do it with Yani.

Talking of ugly, El Negro Sosa is ugly as a hatful of arseholes: he's dark with frizzy hair, a wide flat nose and eyes too far apart. He looks like a pig. He's got lots of nicknames – Bighead, Fatso, Thirteen – but they all refer to the same thing. Truth is, the head on his shoulders is pretty normal, maybe even a bit small for his body. And there's no fat on him. He's hard and sinewy as a knotty wooden cudgel and just as quick to come down on someone. 'Thirteen' is the key. The inches he's got swinging between his legs. The guy's a fucking animal. Even the whores in the barrio are scared of him. He could split them in two. El Jetita calls him Sosa and treats him with respect. Sosa's his deputy.

I pass the General himself as he heads towards the bar. 'What are you doing, *pibe*?' he whispers. 'Sit down, I'll be right back.' I stare at him, but he just carries on walking. These are the first words El Jetita has ever said to me. It's not like I expected a formal introduction. At least now everyone knows everyone. But he better not try giving me orders. Who the fuck does he take me for? One of his toy soldiers?

'Hey . . .' Chueco greets me as I slump into the seat next to him. '*Qué onda?*'

'Yeah, I'm fine, I'm cool . . . you?'

'Sweet. What are you drinking?' he asks, waving Yani over.

'Beer,' I say good and loud so she can hear me.

Halfway to our table, Yani turns and heads back to the bar.

'Give me a cigarette.' Chueco's on the scrounge again.

I give him one and spark one myself. Yani comes back with the beer. The glass is full to the brim, not a millimetre of foam. I give her a wink, but Chueco has to spoil it and says something gross. Yani curls her lips contemptuously, and turns on her heel.

'Jesus Christ, get a load of the arse on that!' Chueco says to me, staring at her as she walks away. I can hardly blame him: you can see her thong through her jeans.

'So what's going on, *loco?*' I say, changing the subject.

El Jetita sits down and starts chatting quietly to Fat Farías and Rubén. One of the few 40-watt bulbs in the bar hangs directly over the three heads. The shrunken pool of light barely extends beyond the table. It looks like a conspiracy. El

Jetita is talking fiercely and waving his hands. Rubén manages to get a word in from time to time and Fat Farías just nods. I'm feeling jumpy.

I look at Chueco and ask him again what's going on.

'We're on a roll, that's what's going on, *viejo*,' he says. 'The lean times are behind us.'

'What are you talking about, *loco*?'

'I'm talking about business. The General there has offered us some work.' He points his cigarette at El Jetita. 'Both of us,' he says as though he hadn't made it clear already.

I take a long slug of beer, necking half the glass so I don't have to answer, and take a couple of drags on my cigarette.

'I told him about your mad skills with a strap and he was really impressed, so you're in.'

He takes a last drag on his cigarette, stubs it in the ashtray and blows the smoke in my face with a triumphant smile.

'Don't mention it,' he says arrogantly. 'Anything for you.'

'Oh, yeah, sorry . . .' I play along. 'Thanks, *viejo*! I'm really fucking grateful.'

'What's the fuck's with you? Play your cards right, you might get your gat. You should be made up.'

'Well, I'm not. I'm out of here. I don't trust that fucker.'

'You chicken, Gringo?'

'Fuck you, Chueco, and fuck your *mamá*,' I whisper through gritted teeth so as not to be overheard. 'I'm not some punk bitch. I just don't trust the guy. You retarded or just dumb?'

'You can't just dump me like this, Gringo.'

'What? Like I owe you something?' I cut him dead.

Chueco arches one eyebrow likes he's the lead actor in some soap. And it's true, I do owe him. I owe him for keeping his mouth shut. And I've been paying him back for years now. There's no way to keep score with this shit, but recently I'm thinking that maybe I've paid my debt. I can't be expected to put up with Chueco's crap for ever just because once upon a time he kept shtum. Sooner or later, the debt's got to be paid. Chueco's taking advantage. And it's not like it was a big deal.

It's ancient history. When we were kids, we wanted to pull off something big, but the plan completely backfired. We'd bought half a key of weed to sell on to the kids in the barrio, but we didn't even get two blocks before the Feds busted us. We were taken down the station. I got released the next day. Chueco spent three months on remand. He was the one carrying. They wanted to charge him with intent to supply, but because he was a minor – we were fourteen or fifteen at the time – they couldn't make it stick, so in the end he got community service. They made him work for free in the nuthouse up in Zavaleta. Twelve months. From what he told me, he had to do pretty much everything, clean the toilets, hand out pills, sometimes even help hold down some psycho who freaked out. But he made a fair bit of cash selling weed up at the nuthouse.

I suppose he did save me, by keeping his mouth shut. The Feds had me press my fingers on the ink-pad and play the paper piano, then they let me go. Simple as. We were in it together, but the cops assumed he was the dealer. They thought I was trying to buy some weed off him. And since Chueco didn't say much in his statement, nobody corrected the mistake.

'What do you take me for?' he said afterwards when I asked him why he hadn't grassed me up. 'How could I drop you in it? We're *socios*, aren't we?'

But the whole thing hardly made him a superhero. Back then, the Feds were in shit. A couple of months earlier, they'd given some kid a beat down just outside the barrio. They'd picked him up in a raid coming out of a concert and he was found the next day in a ditch beaten to fuck. The other rockers picked up in the raid told the judge the kid had freaked out and the Feds had worked him over good. Walter, the kid's name was. It was in all the papers.

For a while after that the *Federales* treated us with kid gloves. Whenever they stopped us in the street they were almost polite. And that's how it was when Chueco and I got picked up. Every cop was playing good cop. I remember they even read us our rights and reeled off a bunch of legal bullshit, habeas corpus, preventative measures and fuck knows what else. Like they needed to issue a special invitation to drag us down the station.

We were pretty lucky. They didn't lay a finger on me, and I'm pretty sure they didn't on Chueco either, so he can't take much credit for keeping shtum. I'm guessing if they'd touched him, he'd have grassed me up like a shot. No cattle prods, no waterboarding, none of that shit. They didn't even work us over old school.

Chueco must have come up with some bullshit story to save his ass. I'm sure the Feds didn't believe a word of it. But luckily I didn't figure in whatever story he cooked up. Since they couldn't touch him, they had to take his word for it. So they let me go.

That was the end of the story, and the end of the whole Hollywood life of crime we'd dreamed up. We'd spent a month and a half scraping the cash together for that first half-kilo, robbing stereos downtown and selling them on to Rubén for a fraction of what they were worth so that way he'd buy the whole lot.

The first half-kilo was to get the operation up and running. We'd worked out the figures. We'd cut it up, sell it on and use the profit to buy a whole kilo, then two keys, then four and so on. We had it all worked out. Our initial investment would snowball. No one could stop it. But stop it they did. Before it even got started. And the snowball melted and trickled through our fingers.

While Chueco was banged up, I did some investigating. I wanted to find out who'd dropped us in it. Someone told me El Jetita had passed information to the police, and I believed it. He wasn't about to let two kids with half a key fuck up his business. Back then, he had the monopoly on selling weed. Same as he does now, but now he's also got a monopoly on coke, crack, *paco*, acid, pills . . . everything. Well, nearly everything – Rubén deals with the stolen cars and the gambling. Nobody handles the whores. They're run by pimps from outside the barrio. Any working girls in the barrio are part-timers, freelance.

It wouldn't surprise me to find out El Jetita and Rubén are partners. They're pretty tight these days. And it wouldn't surprise me if they're trying to make a move on the whores in the area. It's the only part of the business they don't already control.

But the fact remains, El Jetita grassed us up. The normal thing for him to have done in that situation was threaten us. Shit, by the code of the barrio, he could have capped us if he wanted. Because in the barrio there's no such thing as competition or a free market. Everyone round here knows that. But the backstabbing fucker had no right to do what he did do: turn us in to the Feds. Didn't matter how polite the filth were being after the whole Walter case, they were still the filth.

I don't know if the rumours got back to Chueco. I guess so. I never told him. Why try to pin the blame on someone when we were fucked anyway? But watching El Jetita playing nice with Chueco now, I can't forget he was the one who grassed us up.

'You do know who you're dealing with?' I say without warning.

He must have been following my train of thought because he answers with another question.

'What? You think I'm sitting here sucking my thumb?'

'Just saying . . .'

'Yeah, I know what you're saying. Why d'you think I asked you along?'

'You tell me . . .' I push him, but he just ignores it. He finishes his wine and watches Rubén and El Jetita wheedling Fat Farías. They've got him eating out of their hands. I'm guessing one of them is gently threatening and the other one's offering protection. Same old, same old. Good cop, bad cop, just like the Feds.

Chueco finally comes closer to the table, covers

his mouth with his hand and confides. 'Because the first chance we get, we'll turn him in to the filth,' he whispers. 'Because we're going to stab him in the back, and hit him where it hurts – in his wallet. You don't want payback for what he did to us?'

Truth is, I don't. I got off lightly. But I'm not about to tell Chueco that. He'll think I'm shit-scared, and it's not that. I just don't want any more grief. These guys are vicious bastards. You play them on their home ground, you lose. Better to give them a wide berth. El Jetita's got his own code. He's got the scars to prove it. The guy's a fucking time bomb, there's a bullet out there with his name on it and any day now he's going to find it. I'd just rather he went looking for it on his own.

'You're playing with fire, you know that?'

'*We're* playing, *loco*. A debt's a debt.'

Chueco leans back in his seat, narrows his eyes and stares at me. He's waiting for an answer that's not coming, and he knows why. What am I going to say? He's one step ahead of me.

'So what's the story, then?'

'How do I know? El Jetita's going to come over for a little chat with us. Whatever he says, just say yes. Afterwards we'll work out the details and put one over on him.'

THE CONTRACT

El Negro Sosa is warming a plate in the kitchen. He splits opens three wraps and cuts nine lines of coke with a swipe card. Rubén's tearing sheets of paper from a pad and handing them round to everyone. Everyone's here, but the numbers don't add up. There are seven of us. The seventh is Fabían, a tall, skinny guy with bags under his eyes who looks slow and stupid. I've no idea where he showed up from. I think he came with Rubén, but I'm guessing he's not his bodyguard.

'Come on, Farías, don't be afraid,' El Jetita calls. 'The first line's for you, *socio*.'

Fat Farías pushes his way through the strip curtain and steps into the circle where El Jetita is presiding with the mirror in his hand.

What's with the ritual? I wonder. And what the fuck are we doing here? Chueco, sitting facing me, inadvertently answers with a gesture.

'Thanks, I'll save it for later,' he says, taking a

cigarette from Fabían. He twirls the *negro* like a pencil, gives me a wink and slips it in his jacket pocket. We've got them in our pocket. That's what he thinks. Or at least what he wants me to think.

This whole performance is part of the negotiations. This is how El Jetita seals his deals. And the reason we're here is because there are two parties to this contract. Fat Farías is one, and we're the other. I don't know what the deal is, but I can imagine. If we're going to join El Jetita's army, we have to prove we're hardcore.

Rubén hands Farías a sheet of paper and the fat fucker stares at it, confused, for a couple of seconds, then glances at El Jetita and the penny drops. Using his good hand and the bandaged hand he still has in a sling, he rolls the paper into a straw. El Jetita holds the mirror with the lines of *merca* on it right under Fat Farías's chin. Farías puts the paper straw to his nose and snorts.

'So, *viejo*, what d'you think?' asks El Jetita, clapping him on the back.

'Good . . . fucking good,' Farías says in a nasal whine massaging his nostrils between his fat fingers.

El Jetita does a couple of lines.

'This is good shit. It's not cut,' he says, passing the mirror.

El Negro Sosa is next. He licks his lips. He's nervous. He snorts a line, squeezes his eyes shut, throws his head back and rolls it from side to side like he's trying to crack his neck, then passes the *merca* on without a word. Chueco is next, he's been gagging for his turn ever since this whole circus started, flailing his arms, pinching his nose.

Chueco grabs the mirror in one hand, holds his straw to his nostril but never makes it as far as the coke because a hand snatches the paper straw away and crumples it. The mirror falls and smashes on the floor.

'What the fu—? Gordo, what the fuck are you doing?!' El Jetita roars.

'Chueco, you little shit!' roars Fat Farías. 'You motherfucker, I'm going to fucking kill you!'

With his one good hand, Farías has Chueco helpless. He's twisted Chueco's arm behind his back, up between his shoulder blades, and he looks like he's about to break his wrist. Maybe his whole arm. Chueco's on his knees now, scrabbling to reach round and claw Fat Farías's face with his free hand, but he can't reach. He tries to get up, but Farías twists his arm harder, forcing his face to the ground.

'You snivelling fucking rat! I'm going to fuck you up, you and that other *hijo de puta*,' Fat Farías roars and tries to kick me in the balls. I dodge him and try to make a run for it, but I feel a hand on the scruff of my neck dragging me back.

'Play nice, kid,' El Negro Sosa whispers in my ear.

I try to break loose but he squeezes harder. He's breaking my fucking neck.

'Play nice, *che*,' he growls again.

Chueco is writhing on the ground cursing and howling in pain. Fat Farías is still bellowing threats while El Jetita wades into the chaos and tries to restore order.

'Gordo, stop! Stop a minute. Let the kid go!'

'Like fuck I'll let him go, I'm going to kill the little fucker – this one and the other one.'

'Stop, Gordo, let him go! Calm down.' El Jetita grabs Fat Farías's shoulder.

'These are the fucking kids who robbed me!' Farías carries on screaming. 'I'm gonna kill this fucker.' He twists Chueco's arm viciously, making him howl even louder.

'Chill, Farías,' Rubén intervenes. 'If you want, we'll waste the pair of them, but right now just chill out.'

I see the flash of a gun. Turns out Fabián's not slow or stupid. He's the one who's pulled the strap. I feel a chill run down my spine. And it's obvious I'm limp with fear because El Negro Sosa's hand is suddenly limp too. Farías realises what's going on and gets to his feet, giving one last kick as he does so. Chueco doesn't stop howling until El Jetita drags him up by the hair.

Through the strip curtain I can see Yanina's eyes. I guess she was serving at the bar and came to see what all the screaming was about. From the scene in front of her, and from the terrified glance I shoot her, she must realise things have turned ugly.

'Will someone tell me what the fuck is going on here?' asks El Jetita.

'Don't you get it? These little fuckers are the ones who ripped me off!' says Fat Farías.

'You think I'd get my hands dirty robbing you, you stingy bastard?' Chueco tries to laugh it off. 'Who d'you think you are, fucking Rockefeller?'

And things go his way, because El Jetita laughs, and so does El Negro Sosa. Rubén is still stone-faced. Either Chueco is more cool-headed than I thought, or he's more shit-scared than I am and it's the panic that's making him cunning. I know lots of people who go loopy when they're scared.

'How do you know it was them?' asks El Jetita.

'Cos of the watch.'

'This watch here?' El Jetita is trying to sound reasonable. 'Is this your watch, Farías?'

'Fifteen years I've had that watch – you think I don't recognise it? There's a small crack in the glass near the bottom.'

Chueco looks at the Citizen like he's checking the time, then goes for broke. It's all or nothing. He's paler than the pages of Rubén's notebook.

'Are you saying this is your watch, Farías?' he says angrily. 'This is my fucking watch. I nicked it off a couple of kids yesterday, so it's mine. What the hell's got into you, Farías? You nearly broke my arm, you fuckwit.'

Chueco's a genius when it comes to bullshitting. All we need now is for them to buy it. Fat Farías clearly doesn't believe a word.

'*Hijo de puta*, I'm going to fuck you up . . .'

El Jetita isn't buying it either, but he plays along. He winks at Rubén who's still stony-faced, and reassumes his role as a grown-up refereeing a kids' game.

'Let me see that watch. Where did you get it? Tell me, or I'll end you –'

'I told you, it's mine. I robbed it off a couple of kids yesterday –'

'What kids? Charly's gang?' says El Jetita, gently hinting at where Chueco needs to go with this.

'They were taking the piss –' Chueco says, testing the water.

'You're the one taking the piss . . . I told you to run them out of the barrio, not rob the little fuckers.'

It's like El Jetita has superpowers, like his orders get carried out even before he gives them. Putting pressure on Charly's kids is one of the things he asked us to do a few minutes ago, but now he's taking it for granted that that's what we were doing yesterday. Things are starting to become clearer. I take a breath.

'Give him back the watch, Chueco,' El Jetita says, all paternal.

80

'It's fucking mine, if they stole it from him, too fucking bad –'

'Give it back, *che!*' El Jetita roars, smacking him round the head.

It's all an act, but they're good, really good – even I'm starting to believe this shit. Chueco takes off the Citizen and hands it to Farías like he's only doing it because he has to. El Jetita slaps Fat Farías on the back and explains the moral of the story.

'You see, Farías, what did I tell you? Charly's fucking with both of us. He's stealing customers from me, and he robbed your place. The guy's trying to set himself up on our turf, and if we don't stop him, he'll bury us.'

El Jetita is the one who's trying to set up operations here in the bar and I'm betting it's so he can use the place as a base for his dealing. Charly is the local dealer in Zavaleta. He's been expanding his operation lately. And it's true that his delivery boys have no respect for boundaries. Shit, even I've bought weed from them a couple of times. The prices are better than El Jetita's. But from there it's a pretty big stretch to think Charly is trying muscle in on his turf. There's no way he could do it. He'd have to take down General Jetita and all his top brass first, then co-opt all his middle-ranking officers. The list would be too long. And it wouldn't be like shooting ducks at a fair.

'So what about these two?' Fat Farías can't

81

believe what he's hearing. 'Whose side d'you think they're on, *viejo*? Because I'm telling you, I still think they're the fuckers who robbed me –'

'You dissing me, Gordo?' Chueco jumps up. 'Because I'll break your –'

'Shut the fuck up.' El Jetita cuts him dead and goes back to being the peacemaker. 'You're wrong, Gordo. The boys are working with me. You think I don't know who I've on my team? Chill. You've got your watch back, so stop busting my balls. Now, let's strike camp.'

All the time El Jetita's been banging on, Rubén has been staring at us stone-faced from behind Fat Farías. The others can't see him, but we can. He gives us a wink and runs his finger across his throat.

When the big boss is done talking, we all troop out of the kitchen. Rubén and El Negro Sosa sit at the bar. The skinny runt Fabían heads off. El Jetita stops in the doorway chatting to Fat Farías.

'Let's bounce,' whispers Chueco.

And we're about to leave when El Jetita calls us. He takes a couple of steps towards us with a fuck-off smile tattooed on his face. He's acting all friendly again.

'Kids,' he says in a low voice, 'what can you do with them? You give them a simple little job and they land you in the shit.'

Chueco opens his hands, palms up, raises his

eyebrows, like it's nothing to do with him. I stand there, deadpan. I don't know what little job he's talking about

'You little fucktard.' He starts poking his finger hard into Chueco's chest. 'What, am I speaking Chinese or something? I told you straight up to shake down Farías and make sure you weren't seen and you show up here wearing his watch, rubbing his face in it? What is it, you got shit for brains or have you been sniffing something?'

Chueco clicks his tongue. He shakes his head. He's pale. Everything's starting to fall into place for me. The fifty he was flashing in the bar before we did over Fat Farías wasn't snide like he said it was. It was front money. And fuck knows how much he got for doing the job. The worst thing is, I went along with it and I didn't have a fucking clue. And I didn't get a peso out of it. So that's how it is, Chueco, you lowlife *hijo de puta*. You play me for a fool and you don't even tell me what's going down – you even make me think I'm the one who gave you the idea to fuck Farías over. Have to hand it to you, you played me good . . . until now. Because from now on, you can go fuck yourself.

'A complete balls-up,' El Jetita says like he can read my mind, 'and now Gordo is on to you . . . Dumb fucking kids . . .' he swears under his breath, his jaw clenched so Fat Farías can't overhear.

He stares at us, sparks a cigarette and makes like he's thinking.

'OK, kids,' El Jetita says, the fake smile plastered over his face. The bastard knows how to make someone brick it. 'Let me tell you how this is going to go. I'm going to let this one slide, but I've got you by the balls now, so you'd better do exactly what I tell you, because the first sign of any shit I'm going to rip them off. You get me?'

He turns before we've got a chance to say anything, and heads over to Fat Farías.

We walk three blocks in silence. Me thinking about my shit, Chueco thinking about his. Suddenly, I decide I'm sick of his crap, so I start spoiling for a fight – but I play dumb. I make like I haven't worked out what's going on.

'So, you going to turn the tables on that fat fucker?'

'Shut the fuck up, Gringo.'

'Cos it looked to me like he was the one doing the turning . . . and he turned you out good.'

'Shut your hole!'

'OK. It's fine,' I say. 'I'll be your second in command, OK? You lead the way and I'll follow . . . you piece of fucking shit!'

HAND IN THE FIRE

'So tell me, gunslinger,' I taunt Chueco, 'why didn't you pull the gat when Fat Farías was bitch-slapping you?'

It's rare for Chueco to be the one to back down. Usually, however fucked up the situation, he acts first and deals with the consequences later. Luckily this time it was the other way round. If anyone had known he was strapped, the whole thing could have turned into a shitstorm and there'd have been a bunch of collateral damage. And when you've got people firing at random like that, there's nothing you can do, the bad guys always win.

Actually, I don't really give a shit why Chueco bottled it – I'm only asking him to wind him up, force him to show his cards. But he doesn't.

'Because I left it at home, asshole,' he says. 'You think if I'd been strapped I would have let that greaseball get up in my face like that?'

'You left it at the squat?' I say, toying with the

bottle of beer. It's funny hearing him call the
skanky crackhouse he's bunks at home.

'Yeah. Why?'

'Nothing.' I take a long swig, finish the bottle.
'So you're saying you *used* to have a gat.'

'Are you bad-mouthing my crew, *loco*?' He boils
over suddenly like milk. 'D'you ever hear me
bad-mouth your whore mother?'

He's riled. I'm laughing so hard I'm starting to
choke. I can feel beer bubbles up my nose . . .

'It's not like you could – you never knew her . . .'
I say, stifling a sneeze.

'No, but I know all the johns who used to fuck
her. Your *mamá* would do anyone with a pulse!
She'd turn tricks for two pesos. She could suck a
fire hydrant dry and leave it clean as a chicken
bone. You know what they called her? Deep
Throat . . .'

'Keep talking, Chueco, and you'll be shitting
teeth.'

He's the one laughing now. I say nothing, reach
into my trouser pocket to fish out my cigarettes.
Chueco nearly jumps out of his skin. He thinks I'm
about to shank him.

'Chill, Chueco. It's cool,' I say, shaking out a
cigarette. 'I was only asking about the gun.' I pick
the empty beer bottle off the ground and hand it
to him. 'Here. Your round.'

Chueco heads off to the kiosk fumbling for

change in his pockets and I sit back down on the pavement.

First time I challenge him on anything and the *loco* goes off on one. Chueco defends his tribe like they're his own flesh and blood. Obviously in that rathole he lives in he's found the family he never had. Well, if he's prepared to put his hand in the fire for them, let him. I wouldn't. The way things are these days, I wouldn't leave a gun lying around anywhere, definitely not in a crackhouse like that. Too many people hanging around, coming and going, crashing overnight. There's only five full-time residents, counting Chueco – old man Soria who spends all day on his soapbox preaching about shit; Willi, a tall skinny guy – total psycho – no one knows what he does but he's always off his face on something; Pampita, a working girl from up north somewhere. She's pretty fit and all the guys in the squat take advantage. They let her stay in exchange for the occasional free fuck. And then there's El Chelo, a thug I wouldn't trust as far as I could throw him. He used to go out collecting cardboard for recycling but these days he seems to be involved in all the protest marches. That's why he's been lending his cart to Quique.

Chueco comes back with the beer and sits down. He pops the cap with his teeth and hands it to me without even taking the first swig. He's being polite. Personally, I'd rather he was a little less polite and a little more loyal. It's not just about the shit he's got me mixed up in, the stuff he didn't tell me before we did over Fat Farías, what really pisses me off is that he's been cutting deals with El Jetita.

'Fancy going clubbing?' he says, jerking the bottle I've just handed back towards Babilonia.

On the opposite pavement, the queue for the club is getting longer. There's a gang of girls mouthing off.

'Go over and have a word with Julito,' I say, 'but I'm not paying more than five pesos.'

Chueco turns and stares at me. He's used to giving the orders, not taking them. I take the bottle from his hands and neck the beer.

Chueco gets to his feet without a word, crosses the road and elbows his way along the queue. I see him chatting to Julito, the bouncer, for a couple of minutes, then he comes back.

'He'll do us a two-for-one,' he says.

'I'm not putting in more than five pesos.'

'Don't piss me about, Gringo. We go halves, it's eight pesos each –'

'No way,' I cut him off. 'I'd rather lick my own balls.'

'Well, you'll be licking them on your own then. Come on . . . Eight pesos and we get a couple of litres of beer. Cos I'm telling you, with all that sweet merchandise queuing, I'm going in.'

'So go, *loco*. Go on your own. You need someone to hold your hand before you can talk to a chick? I wouldn't do it if you were my kid brother, *che* –'

'Jesus, you've got a mouth on you today. Just give me a cigarette, Gringo, and let's drop this before things turn nasty,' he says, threatening.

'I've only got one.'

Chueco knows I'm lying, but he doesn't say a word.

Just as well. It's all shit. Better we go our separate ways at least for tonight because otherwise we're going to come to blows.

'*Muchachos!*' Santi appears out of nowhere. 'How's things?'

He couldn't have timed it better. He's just in time to defuse the situation. The sliver of air that separates Chueco and me is thick and sweaty. You could cut it with a knife.

'Cool – what about you?' I say to Santi, handing him the bottle of beer. 'What you been up to?'

He takes the bottle, takes a swig.

'Same old, same old. Rabble-rousing and politicking with the kids. We're about to pull a little stunt down by the bridge – you coming?'

'Sure, *loco*. Who are you taking down today?' I feed his ego.

This is all it takes to set him off. Santi's a loudmouth, he's always bragging. But what's worse, he's got a lot to brag about. He's a devious bastard and his stunts always come off.

'Some arsehole thinks he's a big-time dealer. He's got this Fiat that he's pimped out, but you should hear it when he guns the engine, it sounds like a scared fucking kitten. I figure the engine's the same as when it came out of the factory – he hasn't done any work on it. He hasn't got a fucking clue.'

Santi, on the other hand, has got a clue. He's done a lot of work on his own car, a '79 Chevy coupé. He put in a brand-new V-8 engine Rubén sold him. 16 valve. And he polished the piston rims to increase the compression and the power. The thing fucking drinks petrol, but when he floors the accelerator it roars like there's a tiger under the bonnet. And it takes off like a dream.

Chueco chips in and Santi launches into a detailed discussion about motor racing. There's a race coming up, and he's so sure he's going to win he's looking for someone who can bet big so he can take a cut.

By now, I've stopped listening. I'm just focusing on finishing the beer which is still doing the rounds from hand to hand, and finding the right moment to push off.

'Got any weed, Chueco?' Santi asks, trying to make like he doesn't care.

'Only enough for a roach, but tell me how much

you want and I'll bring it down to you at the bridge later,' Chueco says, brown-nosing.

'I don't know . . . just a crumb. I'm good for ten, yeah?'

'If I get a twenty or a thirty, you still up for it?' Chueco tries to persuade him.

Random details from the last couple of days start falling into place again so fast it makes my head spin.

'Sure, the kids will all chip in . . .' says Santi.

I go over to Chueco and whisper, 'Since when did you start dealing, you fucking druggy? Who's supplying the weed? El Jetita?'

'Get the fuck out of here, *loco*' he shouts. He shoves me in the chest and gives a fake laugh. 'All the meat queuing up across the road and you want to go and pay that fucking *crack whore*! Take her!'

'This kid . . .' he says, gesturing to Santi, pretending I've just suggested a threesome with Riquelme, the vilest old whore in the barrio.

Santi doesn't say shit. He doesn't laugh. He's wary. No one likes it when people start whispering in front of them. Me, I don't give a fuck what some car freak thinks of me. But what I do want is to sort things out with Chueco right here and now. I don't know what he's playing at. Little by little I'm getting to see the cards he's holding and I don't like what I see.

I flash him a murderous stare, but Chueco isn't even looking – he won't dare. He's chatting to Santi, any old bullshit, trying to pick up the conversation, making like nothing happened.

I finish the beer, send the bottle spinning in the air and turn to go. If they want to keep drinking they can pay the deposit on the bottle. Turns out it's a lucky throw, the bottle curves straight for Chueco's head, but the bastard's got good reflexes. I hear him swear, hear the dull slap of glass against his hand. I turn and see Chueco holding up the bottle triumphantly. I give him a wink. You might have caught that one, but there's always next time . . .

I walk half a block and then I see her. The last person on earth I want to run into. She's with a couple of friends. I think I recognise one of them from the barrio. I've no idea who the other one is.

'Hey, Yani, what you up to?' I say.

She looks stunning. Her crop top emphasises her tits and shows off her belly button. She's wearing black stockings and a miniskirt that would be a belt if it was any shorter. She's not a girl, she's a sight. She doesn't look anything like the Yani I saw in the bar a couple of hours ago.

'Hey, how are things?' she says. She's trying to act natural, but it's not working.

I kiss her on the cheek. She introduces me to her friends and then waves for them to walk on.

I'm saying whatever comes into my head and she goes along with the pretence until the others have moved away.

'You fucking son of a bitch, Gringo! You did it – you and Chueco.' The tears are threatening to make her mascara run. They're teetering on her lashes.

'I wasn't there, swear to God,' I say, squeezing her hand. With superhuman effort I manage to hold her gaze. I've always been a shit liar, but she's too angry to notice.

'But my old man said . . . So if you didn't . . . ? What's going on between you and El Jetita? What's the guy up to? It was you . . .'

'Calm down, Yani. I swear to you I wasn't there. As for Chueco, well, I wouldn't put my hand in the fire for him. I don't know what they've got your old man mixed up in, but whatever it is, it's bad shit. I can't tell you any more right now. Soon as I find out anything definite, you'll be the first to know. Let's talk later.'

Yani stands, staring at me, mouth half open. I don't give her time to respond. I kiss her on the cheek again.

'Take care. And stay cool, it's all going to be fine.'

After a second I glance over my shoulder to see if she's caught up with her friends or if she's still standing where I left her. She's with her friends.

Good. What's not so good was that thing I said about not putting my hand in the fire for Chueco. It just came out. But it's not like I regret it. If it was disloyal, well, Chueco can just chalk it up for all the times he owes me.

BLUFFING

Mamina's voice wakes me. She's talking to someone, but it takes me a while to work out who it is because they're crying. It's Ernestina. I try and eavesdrop while I'm getting dressed but I can't work out what they're on about. The conversation drops to whispers and one or other of them sighing. It must be late, though I can't work out what time it is. The sky is overcast.

I come out of my room to find Quique sitting on a chair in the kitchen with a sports bag at his feet. It looks empty, but I'm betting there's a change of clothes inside – probably the only change of clothes he's got. He's going to be staying here. Don't need anyone to tell me to work that out.

Ernestina is leaning in the doorway, sobbing silently. Her nose is red, her eyes puffy. She's a mess. She looks whiter than a freshly sheared lamb and all crumpled up inside like a piece of paper.

Mamina has her hands on her shoulders to hold her up.

'Morning . . .' I say.

Mamina says good morning, but Ernestina doesn't even react. Quique barely looks at me. Walking behind his chair to get to the hotplate, I tweak his ear.

'Hey, *viejo*! What you up to?'

'How's it going?' I say. 'You had breakfast?'

Quique nods, doesn't say anything. There's not much to offer him anyway. I put the kettle on the hotplate.

'He's staying here for a couple of days,' Mamina confirms, 'so I want you to keep an eye on the kid.'

'No problem, *abuela*,' I say.

But she's not listening. She's stroking Ernestina's shoulder, whispering to her, trying to comfort her.

'What's going on?'

'Her daughter, the little one, she was taken to the children's hospital yesterday,' Mamina says, looking over her shoulder at me. This is all she needs to tell me.

'Your kid sister?' I say to Quique. 'What's her name again . . . ?'

'Julieta.'

'What happened.'

'Dunno . . . Her eyes went all white and she was jerking around . . .' As he tells me, Quique starts twitching his head and his body to show me what it was like.

Convulsions, I think as lightning flares outside on the street, lighting up the kitchen like a flashbulb.

'What's wrong with her?' I ask loudly so Mamina will have to answer.

And she does. A single word, as the roll of thunder finally comes. I don't so much hear the word as guess it. Meningitis.

I feel it like a blow to the back of my head. There's another flash of lightning, but this one seems to burst behind my eyes, and the white snapshot it burns on to my brain is of the worm-ridden doll.

The tiny kitchen window slams open and a gust of wind blows in. Cold and damp. I latch the window closed, listen to the random clatter of rain on the corrugated-iron shacks. Raindrops big as stones. I stare out, breathe evenly, the rain starts and stops, can't seem to make up its mind. Doesn't matter, summer's over now.

'Gringo, we're going to go before it starts bucketing down,' Mamina says. 'I'm going with Ernestina to the hospital.'

'That's fine, *abuela*, I'll take care of Quique.'

'Where's the umbrella?' she asks, Ernestina clinging to her arm.

'What umbrella?'

'The big black one, *m'hijo*, what else would I mean . . . ?'

I don't know what she's talking about. It worries me to think about Mamina getting senile, but I can't rule it out. She's getting old.

'I've never had an umbrella, Mamina. If it rains, I get wet . . .' I say without malice.

She stands, staring at me strangely, then finally says, 'Never mind, forget it. We're heading off . . .'

Quique doesn't say a word. Nor do I. I brew up a couple of *mate*s and stare out at the rain. It's falling hard now. Quique sighs, eyes fixed on the parallel streams gushing from the gutters around the eaves. I make him a sweet *mate* and he takes it. The wind whips at the ribbons of the strip curtain. It's cold, but I don't want to close the door. With only the milky light from the tiny kitchen window, we'd be standing in the dark. And there's nothing more depressing than having to turn the lights on in the middle of the day.

'Can we put the TV on?' Quique asks, handing the empty *mate* cup back to me.

'We haven't got a TV, champ. Hadn't you noticed?'

He opens his eyes wide in surprise. He doesn't believe me, but it's the truth. I can't be bothered explaining that Mamina pawned it at the first possible opportunity when she needed cash. That was a couple of years ago. She never redeemed the pledge. She said what with the rubbish on TV, we didn't need it, that we'd been better off selling it. I guess she was right.

'But we've got a radio,' I say to cheer him up. 'Want me to put it on?'

'Naw . . . Leave it. There's never any good tunes this time of day. It's just random shit.'

'Your call, *viejo*! But you're pretty random yourself.'

He doesn't reply. We sit in silence for a bit. I make some more *mate*. Sweet for him, bitter for me. Quique gets up and goes to the door, still clutching the *mate*, pushes aside the strip curtain and stands staring out at the rain.

'Hey, *loco*, that thing's not a baby's bottle.'

He hands me back the *mate* and starts nosing round the place. I don't know what he's looking for. Hardly matters, there's not much here he'd be interested in.

'Got a pack of cards?'

'On the mantelpiece next to the cockerel.'

The glass figurine of a cockerel has been sitting on the mantelpiece covered in dust for a thousand years. Someone – I don't remember who – brought it back from a holiday on the coast. It's a bit tacky but at least it's useful. Its tail feathers change colour with the weather. I'm not sure whether it's the humidity or the pressure but the cockerel is never wrong. A blue tail means clear skies. Purple means changeable, so even if the sun is peeking over the horizon, I know it'll be drizzling by the end of the day. Right now it's pink.

Quique reaches up and takes down the pack of cards. He gets the deck out of the box and checks it carefully. Looking for marked cards, I suppose. He doesn't find any. He gives me a wink, sits down again and starts shuffling. He's certainly not clumsy.

'Cut,' he says to me, slapping the pack down in the middle of the table.

I cut.

'What do you want to play?' I ask. '*Casita robada*?'

'That's for little kids,' he says.

'We can't play *truco*. With only two people it's more boring than sucking a nail,' I say as he deals the second card.

Quique gives me a smile and keeps dealing. Five, six, seven cards. He puts the pack in the middle of the table and turns over the top card. This is the last thing I need. I hate *chinchón*. It's a wanker's game. I spent a whole fucking summer playing it while I was trying to get into La Negra Fabiana's knickers. *Chinchón* was the only way I could think to spend time with her. She was obsessed with it. We spent whole afternoons playing never-ending games and I never got anywhere with her. Afterwards I'd jerk off furiously under the bridge by the river.

'Bluff, Gringo. Don't you know how to play Bluff?' Quique says, seeing I'm confused.

'I think so, let's see if I remember . . .'

'You have to discard sets of trumps or cards of the same value,' he explains, 'and if you think the other player's lying you shout Bluff! The first person to get rid of all their cards wins.'

I call trumps: cups. Quique puts down three cards and picks up a card from the pack. He doesn't look like he's bluffing. Me, I'm lying like a politician. And he's letting me. I'm down to only two cards when Quique shouts Bluff. He turns over my last card and I have to pick up the whole discard pile. We start again. Swords are trumps. I use a four to change suit to coins. It seems like a good idea since I picked up the discard pile, but it doesn't turn out that way. Quique discards two, as if the trumps he didn't have earlier have magically multiplied. He has only one card left. I call Bluff and Quique gives me a devious smile. He wasn't lying. He had to be bluffing earlier, even when he picked a card up from the pile and looked disappointed. Otherwise it doesn't make sense. We keep playing and he keeps picking up cards and then on the fourth discard he wins the hand.

I'm annoyed now, so I start really playing, but it's useless. Quique wins three hands in a row and just as I'm about to win the fourth, he snatches victory from the jaws of defeat. I've never been good at lying, which means when I do lie there's a sort of logic to it. Quique's lies are random and there's no tic, no sign he's doing it. It's impossible to catch him at it because he always keeps a scrap of truth up his sleeve in case he's challenged.

He's more devious than I thought. The kid's giving me lessons now, and that really does bust my balls. Then something occurs to me. Half an hour later the water for the *mate* is cold and I use that as an excuse to throw in the towel. It's still overcast, but it's stopped raining.

'You hungry?' I ask, putting the kettle on the hotplate again.

'Bit.'

'Why don't you go and get yourself a *choripán* at Fat Farías's place? I'll give you a couple of pesos. Hang around with the other kids for a bit, keep your eyes peeled and your ears open, then come back later and tell me everything.'

'Is this some kind of deal, Gringo?'

'Some kind, yeah,' I say and give him a five-peso note.

'Done deal,' he says, waving the money.

'And I want to know everything. Who's there, who goes in, who comes out . . . what they're doing . . .'

'You smoke, don't you?' he says just as I'm about to spark up my first cigarette of the day.

I give him a cigarette and Quique heads off.

I go outside and watch him walk down the street. The wet ground gleams like it's wrapped in plastic. Quique moves slowly, avoiding the puddles so he doesn't slip. The wind is still blowing hard. It's cold.

DRAWING A BLANK

I prowl the house like a cat in a cage. There's no reason for me to stay at home, but I've got nowhere to go either.

I pick up the whale book and sit in the kitchen reading. I grip the pages tightly so the money and the note with Toni's address don't fall out. That's where I leave them. I still don't know what I'm going to do.

I suspect Ishmael's a bit of a queer, but I kinda like the guy anyway. While he's waiting to get a position on a whaling ship, he spends a couple of nights at an inn in Nantucket. He shares a bed there with a wild man, a harpooner. A cannibal from the Pacific islands with tattoos all over his body. Queequeg his name is. This guy prays to a little wooden god he keeps in a box, and sleeps with his harpoon. It's difficult to work out what the harpoon would look like, because Ishmael describes it as a huge tomahawk pipe. Thing is,

Ishmael and the cannibal share a smoke, get friendly and maybe get frisky because the book says they're like this cosy loving couple.

Eventually they find the *Pequod*, a whaling ship preparing to set sail, and they sign on. The bit about all the preparations goes on and on. Obviously, in those days, a ship could be at sea for years at a time, so you had to prepare for everything. If you ran out of salt or *mate* in the middle of the ocean, you were fucked. It's not like you could pop down to the corner shop and buy some more. I suppose it makes sense but I'm getting a bit pissed off with all these preparations. I've been reading for over two hours and no one's even mentioned a fucking whale.

My stomach starts to rumble, but I go on drinking *mate*. I can't face food. I spark another cigarette and go on reading.

Anyway, finally, they set sail. The first week, the old captain – his name's Ahab – doesn't show his face. He spends all day every day shut up in his cabin. By the time he finally decides to come on deck under cover of darkness, they're out on the open sea. He rants away on the poop deck for a while and throws his pipe overboard. The old guy's fucked in the head. You can see it in his eyes, in his face. He's got this scar that runs right across his face from his forehead to his jaw. Got it from an axe wound. And he's got a peg leg. Made of ivory,

Ishmael says. From the jawbone of a whale. Where were we? Anyway, the story is that Moby Dick, the great white whale, bit off his leg and the old guy is looking for revenge. He's completely obsessed.

Another night, the old guy gathers all the crew on deck and gives this long speech, telling them they're going to sail right round the world to find this whale if they have to. And he takes out a gold doubloon and nails it to the mainmast and promises it to the first sailor who sights the whale. Anyway, the crew go apeshit and they're all up for hunting Moby Dick. All except one. Starbuck, the first mate, rebels and gets up in the old guy's face. Ahab intimidates him and eventually the guy backs down. Ishmael makes him sound like a wimp, but I figure Starbuck is right. They're out there to hunt *whales*, not just chase one particular whale round the world, and a motherfucker of a beast to boot. It's all about making money. It's not worth risking everything just so some old guy can get his revenge.

Anyway, just when the story's getting good, Ishmael goes off on one. He's done this to me two or three times already. Makes me want to wring his fucking neck. When they first set sail, he went into this whole riff about whaling and what life at sea is like. And when we meet old man Ahab for the first time, he started listing all the types of whale there are in the ocean: Greenland whales, sperm whales, killer whales and I don't know what all. Now he's going on about what colour Moby Dick is. It's good on one hand, because you learn a lot of stuff. Like for instance that they boil whales and turn them into barrels of oil. Or that what brought in the most cash was whale spunk. Back when they didn't have electricity, they used it in lamps like it was kerosene. What he doesn't tell you is how the fuck they extracted the spunk. It's not like they could give the whale a handjob . . . Be pretty difficult anyway, seeing as the whale would be dead.

Problem is, it takes him like twenty or thirty pages to tell you all this shit and you lose the thread of the story.

Anyway, at this point, Ishmael is banging on about the whiteness of the whale and talking so much bullshit you want to end the little fucker. According to him, what's scary about Moby Dick isn't the whale's size, or the hulking wrecks of ships it leaves in its wake – what's scary is the fact that it's white as milk. He's not freaked by the fact the whale's a vicious motherfucker. What terrifies him is the opposite: that it looks so innocent. Pure as a baby lamb.

I give up on Ishmael's ramblings and go hunting for something to snack on. But there's nothing in the place. Half an onion, an empty pack of polenta and a packet of rice that's almost full. I boil up a couple of handfuls of rice with the onion and eat it out of the saucepan. It burns my tongue and the roof of my mouth. With a bit of tuna or a tomato it would be tasty, but on its own it tastes of nothing. White rice is good for one thing and one thing only: killing your hunger.

I laugh at this, because it's like Ishmael's bullshit ramblings are rubbing off on me. My mind is blank. Like it's full of smoke. All I can think about is white. I remember how blindingly white the Portuguese guy Oliveira's house used to be in the sunshine just after it had been whitewashed. It stayed that way for a while. Me and a bunch of kids used to sneak into his garden when he was having a siesta and eat his plums. We'd throw the maggoty ones against the wall. Some little shit even smeared DIRTY PORTUGUESE on the back wall in cowshit.

I think about Albino too, a bull mastiff that belonged to Zaid the Turk. Beautiful animal but vicious. Zaid always had him muzzled, but that didn't stop the dog mauling every living thing it came across. Didn't matter whether it had feathers, scales, fur or a baby's dummy, Albino would go for it. Even Zaid, who fed him, wasn't safe. The dog tried to chew his hand off a couple of times. He was seriously dangerous. But he made Zaid a packet in the dog fights. He was champion of Zavaleta. People would come for miles to see him fight. In the end he had to be put down. He chewed the arm off some kid in the barrio. It was lucky they managed to pull him off when they did, or he would've eaten the kid whole.

White was also the colour of our school smocks. Especially on Monday mornings when we'd show up all smart, hair combed, smocks freshly washed. The weird thing was the kids with the whitest smocks were usually the ones who were starving. It was like you could eliminate poverty with bleach, scrub out stigma with soap. Whiten it in the sun with salt and lemon juice if necessary. My school smock was only ever white until I got into a fight, and I got into fights pretty much every day. Later on, when some moron ripped one of the pockets and Mamina gave me a good slapping, I got in the habit of taking my smock off before lashing out.

I give up on Gringo's ramblings too, as I swallow the last mouthful of rice, and I head out. It's getting dark. It's drizzling. Since Quique hasn't come back to give me the lowdown, I head straight along the alley towards the station, cross the bridge over the riverbed and come out onto the narrow street by Fat Farías's bar.

About fifty yards away from Farías's place I see Quique hanging with a gang of kids. Five or six budding delinquents sitting under the eaves of Tita Cabrera's shop sheltering from the rain, passing round a beer can. I know that what's in the can isn't beer, but still I say to the one cradling it in both hands, 'Hey, give me a swig.'

109

'A swig!' shouts some kid sitting next to Quique who's clearly off his face and that sets off a belated peal of laughter.

I humour them for a couple of minutes, then jerk my head for Quique to follow me. We move away a couple of feet and then suddenly I start coming on like a parish priest. Like a big brother. I regret it the minute I open my mouth.

'What the fuck are you doing sniffing that? Smoke spliff if you want to. Don't you know glue fucks up your brain cells?'

Quique looks at me seriously, closes one eye so he's not seeing double, or triple, then with one finger he draws a circle in the air around my face then points it at my nose. I know this trick; you do it to get things to stand still when you're tripping.

'Life fucks up your brain cells, Gringo,' he says in slow motion. 'Quit busting my balls . . .'

I light a cigarette as he stands there, swaying on his feet, his bottom lip hanging down like a ventriloquist's dummy. All that's missing is the drool.

'Find out anything for me?'

'Something and nothing.'

'What?'

'Round noon Rubén and El Jetita had lunch with the police commissioner from Zavaleta,' Quique says slowly, chewing every word, his

tongue thick and furry. 'Farías cooked an *asado*
and the daughter served. Kicked everyone out of
the bar – even El Negro Sosa, who got a bit
mouthy, and that skinny guy who's always hanging
with Rubén.'

'So what did they talk to the Fed about?'

'No idea. You think they let me stick round for
decoration?'

He's right. Stupid fucking question. Though he's
talking in slow motion and his eyes are blank,
Quique sounds more articulate than ever.

'What else?'

'In the middle of the afternoon, the Fed left and
everyone else came back. El Jetita played cards
with his mates and Chueco came by a couple of
times to talk to him. The second time with that
dark-haired girl he hangs with.'

'Pampita?'

'Yeah, that's her. I didn't see her come out.'

'What about Chueco?'

'Dunno.' He scratches his head, closes his eyes
like he's concentrating. 'He did some kind of deal
with El Jetita, but I couldn't hear what they were
saying. They were too far away. After that I saw
him hanging around out here. Looked like he was
dealing . . .'

'Weed?'

'Coke, too.'

'You sure, Quique?'

'What the fuck's with you?' he says to me. 'It's like your face is made of plasticine.'

'So the other girl, she's still in there?' I say, changing the subject.

'Who?' he asks, confused.

'Yanina.'

'Nah, she fucked off about half an hour after the cop left.'

Quique closes his eyes again and brings a finger to his temple like he's putting two and two together, or trying to work out some code. After everything he's told me – 'Something and nothing,' he said – I'm starting to think sniffing glue has turned him into a prophet or a medium. I'm wired now and I ask him what he makes of everything.

'What the fuck do I know, Gringo?' he says. 'My mind's a fucking blank . . .'

And just as the prophet seems about to come out with a revelation, Quique spirals into glue psychosis and starts coming out with all sorts of shit, telling me that the puddles and the street lights have been sending him messages and they're not good.

'I just give you the gen. You have to work out the conclusions,' he says finally.

And that's the last more or less coherent thing I get out of him.

ON A MERRY-GO-ROUND

I call and call. No one picks up. And when they do, I
wind up talking to myself and the line goes dead. I put
another coin in and get an engaged tone. Without
hanging up, I dial again so the fucking phone doesn't
swallow the money, and when I finally get through I
push another two coins into the slot. The last of the
change from doing over Fat Farías, not counting the
three big bills I've got stashed in the whale book.

'Hello?'

'Hi, Cristina?'

'Who's this?'

'El Gringo, friend of Toni's. Could you give him
a message for me?'

'Sure, shoot . . .' I find it difficult to imagine her
from her voice, but she seems like a girl who
doesn't bullshit.

'Tell him "Mamina says you're dead to her. She
won't say why, but I don't like it. If we're going to
work together, I need to know what went down first."'

Just say it like I said it. He'll know what I mean.'

'No sweat. He's coming by tomorrow to pick up some alpaca, I'll tell him then.'

'Thanks.'

'You're welcome,' she says, polite but curt, and she hangs up.

The call didn't even take a minute, but the phone doesn't spit out any change. I give it a couple of whacks, but nothing. I'm about to kick it, when someone grabs my shoulder.

'Hey, *loco*, cut it out! Don't go fucking up the only payphone in the barrio! If there's an emergency, someone's going to have to run all the way to Zavaleta to call the fucking fire brigade . . .'

'And since when did you start giving a shit?' I say to Chueco, who's standing behind me looking shifty.

'Since we started playing with fire, *loco*,' he says sarcastically. His eyes are glittering. But it's not the hard glitter of coke. He looks drunk. 'Where you been, Gringo? I've been waiting round for you all day. We've got a little job on . . .'

'Well, let's do it now,' I play along, all friendly and shit, 'after all, at night all cats are grey.'

'Come on. Charly's kids are headed down to the park by the station. I just saw them.'

'I'm guessing you're strapped?'

'Too fucking right,' he says, flashing me the butt of the gat sticking out of his belt.

We head straight down the street by the evangelical church, an old converted animal-feed warehouse decked out with neon lights. On Sunday nights the place is heaving. You can hear the pastor singing and shouting. The evangelicals pitched up in the barrio years ago now, but they're still hunting for fools. Even Mamina, who's no fool, was hooked for a while. But soon as they asked for money, she told them where to go.

Chueco can't fucking shut up. He's explaining stuff to me, telling me about his plans. How we're well in now. We've fucked over El Jetita and got away with it, and when we get him to trust us, we'll skewer the fucker big style. I play dumb. I nod and agree with everything he says but I'm not buying it. Chueco's already fucked me over. He's only in it for himself. When it comes down to it, I wouldn't be surprised if I was the one who got shafted instead of El Jetita.

As we come to the park, Chueco asks, like he doesn't give a shit, '*Che*, Gringo, you been in touch with Toni?'

My head starts spinning like a busted merry-go-round, the little wooden horses flying off as it whirls. I don't like coincidences. Never did. I don't like them because I don't believe in them. Either Chueco was listening in while I was on the phone or whatever's going down is more complicated than I thought.

'No, why?' I play dumb again.

'Nothing . . . El Jetita asked about him this morning and I said I'd ask you. Turns out Toni was one of his men until things got fucked up, and now he wants to bring him back into the gang.'

'I thought Toni got himself killed?'

'No, that's bullshit,' Chueco explains. 'El Jetita says the fool's doing arts and crafts somewhere out in the Delta.'

The whole conversation rings about as true as a 32-peso piece. I don't know who's the bigger fool in all this, me or him.

'So why not just ask me himself, instead of getting you to do it?'

'What do I know . . . ?' He dodges the question. 'You know El Jetita, he's weird as fuck.'

The merry-go-round in my head is still spinning out of control. Every little blind horse that flies off is one more unexplained loose end in this fucking tangle: why did Toni have to disappear in the first place? And why can't he come back (because those two things have got to be related)? Why doesn't Mamina trust him? Why is El Jetita so interested in Toni all of a sudden, and what the fuck is Chueco doing caught up in this mess . . . ?

The little horses fly off and shatter blindly against a wall of steel.

'Hey, there they are,' says Chueco. 'Let me do the talking.'

Charly's dealers are sitting along the side of the

path drinking a beer. We rush over to them like we're desperate to score.

'*Qué onda?*' says Chueco.

'What you looking for?' El Negrito Silva says, getting up.

The other kid stays sitting. His name's Medusa. We've known him our whole lives. But when you're dealing, no one's got a name, that's the rules.

'Depends what you're selling.'

'Whatever you're jonesing for, *loco*,' Medusa says, still not getting up. 'We've got everything.'

They're just kids, can't be older than Quique, but when it comes to dealing, they're pros. They've been running deliveries in the barrio for a couple of months now. Charly's using them as an advance party to expand his business. And if things go wrong . . . well, they're cannon fodder. That much is clear.

'Viagra?' Chueco says, completely deadpan.

Silva looks at me and the smile on his face vanishes.

'Don't piss me around, shithead.'

'I'll give you shithead, you little motherfucker,' Chueco says, pulling out the strap. 'Now be good little boys and empty your pockets.'

Little Medusa jumps to his feet and reaches for his belt.

'Look out!' I shout, grabbing the kid's wrist with both hands before he can pull his gun. With his free hand Medusa grabs the hair at the back of my neck.

'What the fuck d'you think you're doing, you little shit?!' Chueco says, shoving the gat into the kid's ear, wedging his head between the gun and my shoulder. But Medusa keeps struggling. The seconds tick past. I'm buzzing on adrenalin. I'm shitting myself.

'What are you doing, guys?' Silva says, his voice calm. 'You're gonna get yourselves in serious shit.'

'Shut your hole, Negrito, and show me your fucking hands,' screams Chueco. 'Don't fucking move or I'll end you, and I'll cap your little friend too if he goes for that strap!' Chueco is bricking it. I can't see it, but I can feel it.

I'm staring at the sky. Black. Medusa has my head jerked back, tugging at a fistful of my hair like he's about to rip it out. My neck hurts like fuck. But the difference in our ages works in my favour. I've still got both hands gripping Medusa's wrist to stop him pulling the gun holstered in his pants. I force his wrist down hard, pressing the barrel into his balls. If he keeps this up, he's going to blow his chances of passing on the family name.

'Let it go. Let it fucking go,' I say, and the sound of my own voice scares me shitless. I sound calmer than El Negrito Silva. Must be fear. 'Cap him, Chueco, don't piss about, just do it . . .' I say, at the same time praying that neither of them gets a shot off.

I don't know if Chueco thinks I'm serious, but I

suddenly feel Medusa's head slam harder against my shoulder. Chueco's drilling a hole in his ear with the gat. Since everything with Medusa seems to go in one ear and out the other, I'm probably looking at a bullet in the shoulder. But maybe he is listening, because the threat seems to work. He goes limp. I wrestle the gun from him and step back. It's an automatic.

'Fucking kids . . .' says Chueco, letting out all the air in his lungs. He's pale. To calm himself, he gives Medusa a kick in the stomach. 'And one for you too, you little hood,' he says, kicking Silva in the back of the head. El Negrito gags, swears and swallows snot. Medusa is still doubled over on the ground, one hand on his belly and the other on his mutilated ear.

'Now these two little shits are going to listen to me and listen good. First you're going to make a nice little pile of everything in your pockets, right down to the last toffee, on this . . .' As he talks, Chueco takes off his jacket and lays it at Medusa's feet like a blanket. 'Come on, do it!' he says, and gives another slap to El Negrito Silva who's still snivelling.

When Medusa said they had everything, he wasn't shitting. On to the jacket they toss wraps of coke, tabs of acid, lumps of hash in every shape and size, rocks of *paco*, a dozen blister packs of pills of various colours, and a lot of cash in small bills.

'I said everything down to your last Rolo, or are you trying to piss me off?' Chueco growls, seeing them stop.

The kids keep pulling wraps out of their underpants, their shoes, from behind their ears . . . it's like Mandrake the Magician.

'Incredible . . . these kids are a walking pharmacy,' Chueco says excitedly. The gleam is back in his eyes; I'm guessing fear sobered him up pretty quick. Fucking moron. He always had good reflexes, but the first time he decides to play the gunslinger, he shows up off his face. We're lucky Medusa didn't end us both before he had time to react.

'Take a look at this . . .' he says, taking Medusa's gun from me.

He's like a kid with a new toy. A .22 Beretta.

'Careful, Chueco, mind what you're doing!' I yell, snatching the .38 from him.

He turns the automatic over, takes out the clip, slaps it in again and leaves it cocked.

'Right. You know what's going to happen now, kids?' Chueco goes all paternal again. 'I'm going to count to twenty and then I'm going to do a little target practice. I'm not much of a shot, but I figure I'll still hit one of you. Whichever of you gets away should go tell your boss from El Jetita that his little game is over. From now on, any dealing in the barrio is our business. Clear? Any of Charly's people who stroll through the park this side of the refinery won't be strolling back to Zavaleta. And anyone who comes to try and pick up what's left of them will wind up the same way. Are we clear?' Chueco concludes his speech, still turning the Beretta over in his hands. He's in his element. The two kids don't say anything. 'Right, now why don't you little fuckers get running, I want to test this beauty. Have to hand it to you, it's a nice piece . . . On your feet, get moving! One, two, three . . . !'

The two boys take off at top speed down the alley leading to the plaza. Chueco keeps counting, shouting out the numbers. By the time he gets to twenty, the kids are nearly four blocks away. He'd have a job hitting either of them. They start to zigzag. They know all the moves. Chueco fires off a couple of rounds just for the hell of it. Just to make some noise.

He bends down and starts counting the money.

'There's a fucking fortune here, Gringo.' He makes three piles, pushes one towards me and says, 'Here, you take this one, I'll take the other, the rest we hand over to El Jetita like good little boys. What do you say? Same with the dope. Jesus, this is fucking beautiful. There's everything here. Take whatever you want.'

I wad up the pile of money and stuff it into my pocket, pick up a lump of hash.

'For fuck's sake, take something decent, gay-boy. Have you ever seen so much dope in one place .. ?'

'It's cool, I'm fine with this,' I say, nodding to the .38.

'Don't be a smart-arse, Gringo,' he shouts.

I don't answer.

'What, you think you can take my fucking gun just like that?'

'What do you think, Chuequito?' I say, stuffing it into the back of my jeans.

Chueco stares at me with the Beretta in his hands.

'What? You going to shoot me? Better make sure you aim well, because if you fuck up, I'll end you.'

I turn my back and walk away. He hasn't got the balls. At least that's what I'm hoping.

'Gringo. Gringo! Come back, *che*! Don't be such a jerk! Gringoooo!' he wails like a sheep having its throat slit.

I don't even turn. Let him bitch all he wants, the gun's mine. I earned it fair and square for saving his fucking arse. Besides, I'm going to need it. I can see it coming . . . Let him keep his new toy. I've got off the merry-go-round. I'm not spinning any more.

THE CHURNING RIVER

There's a light on at home. Mamina's back. So is Quique. Through the strip curtain I see a steaming bowl on the table. A hand stirs, loads a spoon and disappears. It's the kid. They're talking in low voices. Mamina's probably telling him how his little sister is doing. I don't go in. I walk on up the lane, toying with the lump of hash. I haven't got any skins but it doesn't matter, I use the scrap of paper that's got Cristina's number on it. I keep the bit with the number but smoke part of her name and most of the directions for how to get to Toni's gaff in the Delta. I know them by heart anyway.

I take the last couple of tokes on the bridge over the stream. The water's pretty high right now from all the rain today. The wind's blowing from the east, and the sky is clear. A fat, lazy full moon lights up the water as it rushes. The muddy riverbed must be all churned up.

I chuck a couple of stones, try to skim them on

the water, but they just skip once and then sink. Used to be I could get them to skip six, seven times, all the way across the river. Used to be able to smoke a cigarette right down to the butt without the ash falling . . . Used to. Not now. Now I've got a .38 with six bullets in the cylinder. I counted them. I've got some cash in my pocket and more in the whale book back home, under my mattress. I've got a fucked-up feeling I might lose my balance and fall, and a kind of longing to go to hell.

I swing by Fat Farías's place, but I don't go inside. Chueco's probably gone back to his squat to crash. If not, he'll be inside doing deals with El Jetita. The bar is rammed. I go round and sit in the little courtyard out back where Farías chucks the empty wine barrels and all the rubbish from the kitchen. There's some people in the storage shed at the far end. I know because I can see light coming through the little holes in the corrugated iron. Besides, someone's moved all the crates of beer and fizzy drinks outside. I go closer to the shack and put my ear to the wall. I hear gasps. They're fucking in there.

I slip behind the wall of beer crates and creep towards the kitchen door. I hear the hoarse voice of a famous sports commentator and people shouting. They're showing the highlights from today's matches. That's why the place is rammed: Farías has got a TV in.

The door opens unexpectedly. I take a step back and hold my breath. Between the crates, framed against the light, I see El Negro Sosa. He can't see me. I'm standing in the shadows.

'Pampita!' he yells. 'Time's up!'

He goes back inside, leaving the door half open. I can hear people talking in the kitchen pretty clearly.

'You want me to put the mattress down in the middle of the corridor?' a woman's voice says, husky from gin and cigarettes. I recognise it. It's La Riquelme.

'Obviously – it's not like there's any fucking space anywhere else,' El Negro Sosa says irritably. 'Why, were you planning to make up a camp bed on top of the stove, *vieja*?'

'OK, *papi*, no need to take that tone with me. I was just asking . . .'

'Less of that *papi* shit. It's Señor Sosa to you. You better learn some respect or I'll beat it into you.'

I can imagine him raising his hand. El Negro looks exactly like you'd expect a pimp to look. It's like he was born to play the part.

'When Pampita's next john is done, make up the bed here. I have a client for you, got it?' he explains to old Riquelme.

Two whores in one tiny little room. The space might be tight, but they've clearly got business turning over quickly. El Negro obviously wants to use the kitchen too, but it's really narrow and it's the only way to get out the back.

Right. I've heard enough to have a good idea of the cards he's holding. I'm about to bounce. But just as I'm about to come out from behind the beer crates, the shed door opens. A tall dark-haired guy who looks like he's from the barrio comes out and heads back through the kitchen. The light from the storage shed hits me right in the face. Pampita leans in the doorway, casting a shadow over me, but she can't miss me. The john disappears and I whisper, 'Pampita, Pampita, don't grass me up . . .'

Her hair is a mess and she's wearing a short nightdress. It's old and worn. You can see her dark nipples and the triangle of pubic hair through it. She's got no fat on her – I'm guessing she's doesn't eat much – and her skin is tanned. All the right curves in all the right places. Those *hijos de puta* have got themselves a fine piece of merchandise.

'Gringo,' she starts, 'what you doing here?'

'Shh . . . nothing . . . make like you haven't seen me. What you been up to?'

'Me? Nothing . . . they don't give me time to catch my breath . . .' she says.

And she stops. Like she doesn't want to talk about it. I raise an eyebrow and she says reluctantly,

126

'Been in here since gone noon. I've fucked so many guys I've lost count.'

'What are you bitching about?' I say. 'You must be raking it in . . .'

'No, El Negro handles the cash. Hasn't even told me what my cut is.'

'In that case, I wouldn't hold your breath . . .'

Pampita's eyes well up and catch me off guard. My cynicism disappears faster than a cat about to take a bath. There's an awkward silence and then I ask a question, it's dumb but it's genuine.

'How did you end up getting involved in all this?'

'Your friend Chueco, he's the one who tricked me into coming here. Then, soon as I got here, El Negro started laying into me with his belt. In the end I got tired of being hit . . .' There's another silence then she confirms my suspicions. 'And since then the bastard's taken everything I've got.' Pampita brings a hand up to her arse. She's crying now. El Negro Sosa's really fucked her over.

'I'm not surprised Chueco's involved,' I say. 'Why don't you wait till no one's looking and do a runner?'

'What if they catch me?' she says. She's terrified.

'You have to risk it . . . I don't know what you were thinking coming here, you're never going to make it.'

I feel sorry for her, because she's not stupid. She realises now that just setting foot in Fat Farías's place was a bad move, but I haven't got time to tell her just how bad, to convince her to get the fuck out of here. El Negro's already on his way with the next client. I can hear him telling dirty jokes and the john laughing. I give Pampita a wink, put a finger to my lips for her to keep her mouth shut. She nods and makes a vague gesture, something between an appeal and an acceptance. I sprint across the courtyard and hide behind the half-open door. I don't move a muscle until the conversation dies away as the client goes into the shack with Pampita and Sosa goes back into the kitchen.

The road is covered with a thin slick of mud. Just enough to break your neck. I decide to take the potholed pavement instead. At least there's some traction. The soles of my shoes stick to the few unbroken paving stones. All I have to do is dodge the puddles.

The wind comes in fits and starts, but it's not cold. The night is stifling, humid. The roars of drunks celebrating goals carry from the bar on the wind, fading as I get further away. No one around. Not many lights on. It's late and tomorrow's a work day. What's left of the street light ends here where the tarmac stops. This is where the barrio really starts. A gaping hole in the darkness. The wolf's mouth, as the cool *porteños* call it.

Solitude, crickets, frogs. The soundtrack of fear. If only it would rain in a biblical way, a downpour that would rip the sky open and make the earth thunder. But the only thing thundering right now is my stomach. It wants food. It's been gnawing on fear for hours now. I have to feed it something, even though I don't feel hungry. I walk a couple more blocks down the dirt path of the dark alley and turn down one of the cul-de-sacs by the station. From a distance I can see a light on in Zaid the Turk's place. He's always open. Don't know when he sleeps. Must be the only way to keep the business going.

The Turk set up a stall with what fight he had left in him after his mastiff had to be put down. There wasn't a dog in the world like Albino, he said, and he gave up going to the dog fights. On one of the walls of the shop he's still got a huge photo of the dog in mid-slaughter. It's a blurry, out-of-focus shot, but it says it all. A white form spattered with red standing over a pile of blood and hair.

The Turk spends all his spare time staring at that photo. And he's got a lot of spare time, because he never closes. Sundays, public holidays, three in the morning, Zaid's stall is always open, and he's always standing there, motionless, on

guard. Go figure what he sees in that fucking
photo. Albino's the one should be watching
over him.

And that's how he is when I get to the stall.
Silently grieving over his memories or the spectre
of guilt. What the fuck do I know. Through the
bars of the grill, he serves up what I ask for: five
alfajor biscuits on special offer, a pack of cigarettes
and a bottle of Legui. We barely speak. He gives
me a plastic bag with my change, and I take it
without a word and put what I've bought in it. The
Turk's already sat back down on the bench behind
the counter, eyes half closed, staring at the picture
of the dog. I leave without saying thanks.

I wander around aimlessly, swinging the plastic
bag and stop again by the river. But this time I
don't go onto the bridge. I sit on a pile of rubble
on the bank. The water's still rising. It's moving
like an animal. Swirling and eddying. Washing
away all the garbage.

There's only a sliver of moon visible now in the
gaps between the clouds tumbling across the sky.
Difficult to tell which is moving faster, the river or
the storm.

I peel the foil off the first *alfajor* and eat it
half-heartedly. I wash down the rest with a couple
of shots of Legui. What with the caramel and
sugary quince jelly in the *alfajor* and the sweet
liquor, it's cloying and sickly sweet. But I still feel

the same bitterness inside. I try not to think. I light one cigarette after another, chain-smoking until the bottle's empty. I toss it in the river and it sinks like a stone. I picture it spinning down to the bottom. The riverbed must be more grotty than Pampita's rickety old bed.

LIKE CAT AND DOG

The place looks different with her in it. I hardly recognise it. Her presence transforms it. Either that or I was shit-faced the first time I came in. Though what with the weed and the bottle of Legui I'm not exactly sober right now. I'm feeling more cranked than chilled to tell the truth.

'Come in,' Yanina says, half asleep.

I follow her down the dark hallway. She is framed, silhouetted by the bluish glow from the far end. Her generous hips and her drooping shoulders. Her loose hair. She's wearing a baggy T-shirt as a nightdress. Her feet are bare. Her soles slap against the floor with every step. The glow is from the TV. She's watching a black-and-white movie starring Libertad Lamarque that's old as the hills. She goes over and turns down the volume until the dialogue is an almost inaudible murmur.

'You still up?' I ask. 'Don't you have to be up early for school tomorrow?'

132

'No. Teachers' strike.' She clicks her tongue. 'I couldn't sleep . . .' She blinks at me repeatedly. I notice that.

She sits in a chair facing the TV, curls her legs under her and pulls the T-shirt over them. It's a fraction of a second, that's all, but for that fraction of a second she gives me a flash of her thighs, the curve of her arse, her bare hip that knocks me out. She takes a cigarette from the pack of Lights on the table and sparks it up. She takes a deep drag, blows out the smoke and hugs her knees like she's still cold.

'What was it you wanted to say to me?'

No beating about the bush. Straight to the point. So straight it unsettles me. Something and nothing. What am I supposed to say now?

'Lots of stuff, Yani,' I say, bringing a cigarette to my lips. 'I don't really know where to start.'

I sit down at the table opposite her and she picks up a digital watch hidden behind the ashtray and peers at it in the glow from the TV.

'Start wherever you like, but get a move on, it's late. My old man's going to roll in any moment.'

'I doubt it, the bar is rammed . . .' I say, playing for time. 'He'll be a while yet.'

She frowns, sucks on her cigarette and says, 'Whatever, Gringo. He doesn't like me letting people into the house, and I don't want to take the risk. He can be very overprotective . . .'

'What is it, Yani? Does he hit you?'

This catches her off guard, though that wasn't my intention. I said it without thinking. The answer's obvious. Yani stares at me, her eyes huge and round as a dog that's been beaten slinking back to be petted. She pushes a lock of hair behind her ear and stubs her cigarette out in the ashtray.

'No, but sometimes . . .' She looks away.

She's scared. I realise that. Farías the fat fucker probably beats her all the time. I'm sure he does. It's obvious. You can smell fear, and I can feel her fear prickling my nose. There's an awkward silence. This isn't how I wanted things to go. The whole thing is getting away from me. I clear my throat and light another cigarette.

Yanina stretches out her legs and stares at them for a moment. I lean over the table and stare at them too. They're beautiful. Especially her knees. Her ankles are covered with tiny red marks. Insect bites. Mosquitos, maybe, or fleas, I don't know. But I love them. They're so delicate. She slowly puts on her slippers and gets up.

'You fancy sharing a *mate* –?'

'Sure,' I say before she's even finished the question. She could offer me cyanide and I'd still say yes.

I get up and follow her into the kitchen. She turns the light on, puts the kettle on the stove. It's just as filthy as it was the other night, but a little tidier. There are no burnt saucepans in the sink and the table has been more or less cleared. Yanina reaches up to take down the *mate* gourd and the *yerba mate* from a shelf. I make the most of the opportunity to appraise her arse. I can see she's wearing a thong under her T-shirt. I'm shocked. I'm also horny as hell. Up to this point I've behaved like a perfect gentleman, but I don't know how much longer I can hold out. She gives me a sidelong glance. She knows. Least I think so, because I see her smile with her eyes. She packs *mate* into the gourds and brews it the Uruguayan way, adding cold water first. She strains the gourds in the sink, turns on the tap and lets the water run. The kettle is whistling by now. Before she turns it off I suggest, 'Why don't we add a little something?'

'Like what?' She looks at me like a naughty little girl.

'I don't know, what you got . . . ?'

'Let's have a look . . .' She opens the fridge and stands, staring into it like it was a window at night or a cave filled with shadows. Inside, it's darker than a wardrobe. Unless I mistake, I'd swear it was empty last time.

'You OK with gin?' she says, turning her body, one hand still on the door of the fridge.

'Perfect. Bols?'

'No, Llave.' She bends down, takes out a litre-and-a-half bottle and hands it to me. It's warm.

'You keep that thing turned off to save on electricity or am I confusing a cupboard with a fridge?'

She laughs. And everything's fine between us.

'No, it's on the blink,' she says with an irritated gesture.

I take the top off the bottle, take a sip of the gin and hand it back to her.

'Yech . . . the Llave's a little bitter. Why don't we sweeten it up a bit . . ?' I suggest.

'Hang on, let me see. I think there's honey somewhere . . .' She puts the gin down next to the *mate* and starts searching in the cupboard under the counter. After a while, just as I'm getting impatient and about to tell her not to bother, she stands up again, triumphantly brandishing a bottle.

'Found it!'

She unscrews the cap and tries to push a spoon into it, but she can't. The honey is too old. It's crystallised.

'Let me have a go,' I say, seeing her give up.

I go over to the counter and the scent of her skin hits me like 220 volts. The smell is both fresh and intense. I take the bottle and hold out my hand for the spoon. She presses it against my palm but doesn't let go. I close my fingers around the spoon, and around her fingers. Yanina lets her fingers stay in mine for a moment and our eyes meet.

I carve out a little nugget of honey and let it

drop into the gap between the damp *yerba* and the silver straw, the *bombilla*. Yani does the rest. She adds a large splash of gin and pours on the hot water.

'Help yourself,' she says and passes me the gourd.

It's steaming. It's fucking amazing. I can feel it warming my whole body.

'So, what's it like?' she asks impatiently.

'Lush. Really lush,' I say smiling, staring at her eagerly. I've never been this close to her.

I hand back the *mate* and our fingers brush again. Accidentally or on purpose, makes no odds. She puts another splash of gin in, tastes it. She likes it. She brews another one for me and moves a few inches away. As a precaution. Our fingers are like bare wires, sending out sparks every time they make contact. Live and earth. Difficult to tell which of us is carrying the electrical charge. Doesn't matter.

I lean back against the counter and feel the .38 dig into my kidneys. It's so well holstered, I didn't notice it till now.

As I drink the last of the *mate*, sucking on the *bombilla* until it whistles. I nod towards the fridge.

'Are you going to get someone to come and look at it?'

'They already did . . . It can't be fixed, we'll have to get a new one,' she sighs.

'So how do you manage?'

'I don't . . .'

From the look on my face, Yani can tell what I'm thinking. With all the cash Fat Farías spends on wine, you'd think he could buy her a new fridge, even a second-hand one.

'The old man says he's got three fridges at the bar so he doesn't need another one . . .' she explains.

'No offence, Yani, but Don Farías sounds like a bit of a Neanderthal.'

'A bit?' she says and laughs again, but half-heartedly. Almost bitterly.

I change the subject. We talk about the movie with Libertad Lamarque, about insomnia, about the yowling of cats on heat . . . anything. Anything as long as there's no mention of Fat Farías and his bar. The old man's bar is the eye of the storm. Hers and mine. And just now, we don't want to deal with it. The *mate* is too good to ruin it. So good we keep adding more water. At this stage, we've brewed every ounce of flavour from the *yerba*, and keep adding a little something until we've gone through a quarter of the bottle of gin. Yanina's eyes are shining. Her cheeks are flushed.

I put the *mate* down on the counter and, without warning, grab her round the waist and pull her to me forcefully. She doesn't resist, and I bite her lips. Yani's tongue is dancing in my mouth.

It tastes of gin, of tobacco, of plums, of cough mixture, of rosemary . . . and lots of other things I couldn't begin to explain. But most of all, it tastes of desire. I slip my hands under her T-shirt and run my fingertips over every inch of her arse. She gets goosebumps. Our breathing accelerates. She pulls up my windcheater and my T-shirt, feverishly. Desperately. I cross my arms and pull them both over my head in a single movement. Time is speeding up. Or we're speeding up. I put a hand on the small of her back. I lift her up, turn round and set her on the counter. While I pull the front of her T-shirt over her head and hook it round the back of her neck like a striker celebrating a goal, Yanina unbuckles my belt and opens my fly. The .38 falls, slides into the turn-ups of my jeans and drops to the floor with a sharp clatter.

'Stop, stop . . . did you hear that?' She's nervous.

'I didn't hear anything, Yani,' I lie.

I bite her nipples and she takes my cock in both hands and aims it at the centre of the target like it's her own personal toy. She pulls hard, like she's going to rip it off. With my index and middle fingers, I pull her G-string aside and trace the outline of her lips. Warm and wet. My fingers slip lazily in, opening a path. And I'm inside her. A journey into space. The final frontier. Now she's the one biting. My earlobe. And she's growling. Her tongue is tracing a song in saliva in my ear. I hang onto her hips like they're the anchor for a paper boat in a raging storm. Out of sight of land. On an open sea, one that does not close. The only way is in. And I'm inside her. But the sudden contractions of her pussy as it grips me tight bring me back to earth. She whimpers and digs her nails into my side. Now I'm a trigger. The pain subsides. And I bite. I bite the dust, the last reflex of a man who's been shot.

I give up. I rest my forehead in the cleft between her breasts. The sweat from her skin revives me. She wraps her arms around my shoulders and covers my neck with little kisses. I listen as she gets her breath back. Then with a thrust of her hips, she expels me.

'Just look what you did to me, Catwoman,' I say, showing her the scratches down my side as I pull up my pants.

'What about you, you little dog?' she says, sticking out her lower lip.

There are small purple bruises where I sank my teeth into her. One of them has produced a pearl of blood.

She pulls down her T-shirt and straightens her hair. With the toe of my shoe, I push the .38 under the cupboard. And we pick up the conversation as though we'd never left off.

'He thinks I've got the makings of a madame . . . he wants me to look after his shit.'

'Who? El Jetita?'

'Who do you think . . . ?' she says, irritated.

'I though El Negro Sosa took care of the girls?'
I say.

'Don't talk to me about that slimy bastard. *Hijo
de puta*. He scares the shit out of me. He and El
Jetita both want to fuck me.'

'What does your old man say?'

'Nothing. He agrees with whatever they say, like
he owes them something . . .'

'Money?' I guess.

'Not as far as I know.'

'What was the deal they were doing with the
police commissioner from Zavaleta?'

'He's agreed to turn a blind eye until Charly
and El Jetita sort out the turf war. After that he's
planning on charging them both a "free trade
tax". That's what he called it. Can you believe
that?'

'This turf war, people are going to get shot, Yani,'
I warn her. 'If you stay on at the bar, you could get
caught in the crossfire.'

'Sure, I guess, but what do you want me to do?'

'Get the fuck out of here,' I say.

She looks me in the eye. And the pool of fear in
her eyes threatens to drown me. Our faces are
inches apart.

'What about *papá*? I'm just supposed to
abandon him?'

'He's a big boy, isn't he? He knows what he's getting himself mixed up in –'

'What *they're* getting him mixed up in,' she cuts in sullenly. 'They set things up. El Jetita and all the guys who hang around with him, like you and your friend Chueco for example.'

'I'm not involved in any of this, Yani! Get that into your head . . . ' We're like cat and dog now. The harmony that was between us is completely fucked. 'And just so you know,' I add, 'I'm getting out of here. I'm heading up to the Delta.'

'What are you going to do up there?' Her tone is softer.

'I don't know. Whatever. Something will come up. If you want to come with . . . '

Yanina suddenly laughs, but it sounds forced. She's scared. She wasn't expecting me to come out with something like that.

'And I'm supposed to just quit school when I'm about to graduate?'

'No . . . ask for a deferment and do your exams up there.'

She seems like she's thinking about it, but she doesn't look too convinced. She frowns and gets down from the counter. I get dressed. I bend down, pretending to tie my shoelace and grab the strap.

'You make it sound so easy, Gringo, but it's not that simple . . . ' she murmurs like she's talking to herself.

142

I don't say anything. And she says it again, her eyes vacant.

'It's not that simple . . .'

I take this opportunity to slip the gun into the back of my jeans without her noticing. But Yani's quick. She wises up. And the look she gives me says it all.

RIDDLES

There are things about Mamina I don't understand. All the pointless work she does, for example. But her attitudes too, the way she reacts . . . The more I know her, the less I understand. Right now she's scrubbing the doorstep like she does religiously every other day. Come rain, thunder or hail she scrubs that little patch of concrete until it's spotless. And today's the day.

I listen to her fill the bucket from the outside tap. I watch her through the tiny kitchen window. Through the fog. She splashes out the water and scrubs with her brush. She's stick-thin and getting thinner by the day, getting smaller and more stooped, and still she carries on with every last ounce of energy. And it's not worth a fart. First person walks past and the pavement will be dirty again. The rain has turned the dirt road into a swamp, but still Mamina goes on scrubbing the doorstep. I don't know where she gets the strength.

I put the kettle on the stove and brew up a couple of *mate*s. I bring a sweet one out to her. Just the way she likes it.

'Morning . . .'

'Good morning, *m'hijo*. How did you sleep?'

Like shit, but I don't tell her that. I feel sorry for her. Quique is sleeping in my bed. Like a log. And Mamina took great pains making up another bed for me. A box and a couple of blankets. I went to bed just as it was getting light and woke up a little while later with my back fucked. After that, I didn't get a wink of sleep, though I tried.

'So-so,' I say.

'I'll go over to Ernestina today and ask her to lend me a mattress . . .'

'Don't worry about it, Grandma, you've got enough on your plate with the kid.' She glowers at me like I'd just said something terrible.

'How's the little girl?' I ask in passing.

'Still weak.' She sucks greedily on the *mate* then hands me back the gourd.

I bring her another sweet *mate*, and when I bring her the third she says no thank you. She doesn't want any more. She's frugal even when it comes to *mate*.

Inside, Quique is already up. He's taken some of the hot water from the kettle to brew himself an instant *mate* in a jam jar. He's making himself at home.

'Hey, *compañero*, you could at least ask first!'
'Don't bust my balls, Gringo.'

He grabs two sachets of sugar, tips them into his *mate cocido* and, blowing on the jam jar, wanders over to the shelf where Mamina keeps the radio. He flicks it on, turns the dial till he comes to a station playing 'Sympathy for the Devil', cranks up the volume.

'I thought you were a slum-boy *cumbia* fan?' I say to wind him up.

'I was, and now I'm a Stones fan,' he plays along.
'Since when?'
'Since right now.'
'Fuckwit . . . Why?'
'Meh . . . people change.'
'Do you even know what they're singing about?'
'No, but I still like them.'

I like them too. Particularly this song. I like the drumming. Sounds like *candombe.* But at least I know what the lyrics mean. More or less. Santi, the mad fucker, translated them for me one time when we were in his Chevy. 'Sympathy for the Devil' is all about this guy who's filthy rich and has good taste, but doesn't tell you his name. It's like this game, he wants you to guess his name, gives you a bunch of clues, in case you're thick. The chorus is just 'Who, who, what's my name?' like it was a riddle and he's being all mysterious.

Drinking his *mate cocido*, Quique taps along with his foot. He glances over at me and laughs. He's a strange little fucker. When he's finished, he puts the jar in the sink. I'm still leaning on the counter, still drinking my *mate*. He turns and comes over to me, all mysterious.

'If you want to keep playing the spy game, I'm up for it,' he whispers.

I stare at him, and he stares back. He even raises one eyebrow. Who the fuck does he think he is, James Bond?

'Yeah, why not . . .' I say. 'Just let me know if you see anything out of the ordinary.'

'But the price has gone up, OK? Ten pesos, as long as no serious shit goes down. Otherwise, it's more . . .'

'What? Are you off your head?'

The Stones song fades out and an Argentinian rock song comes on. I spark up a cigarette. Chew the skin on my index finger. Stare out the window . . . Basically, I play dumb.

'I mean, you don't want someone gunning you down, do you?' he says, point-blank.

'I suppose you do?'

'I'm just saying, because if Charly's gang are looking to cap you, I can keep you posted.'

'And who told you Charly's got it in for me?'

'After the shit you pulled with El Negrito and Medusa, stealing his stash, he's not gonna send fucking flowers . . . Or if he does, it'll be for your funeral.'

'Who told you about ripping off the stash?'

'Saw it myself with the two eyes God gave me, *papá*,' he says, making a V-sign and pointing to his eyes.

Someone's done some kind of switch on this kid. This can't be dumb, gentle little Quique . . . I always had a soft spot for him . . . Now I want to strangle the little fucker. He took the whole spy game very seriously. He followed me when I went off with Chueco. Good job he's on my side.

'You are bang out of order.' I've got to stop this in its tracks. 'Is it me, or are you trying to fuck with me?'

'No way, Gringo, I'm on your side.'

'I'm just saying, because looks to me like you're taking the piss . . .'

He thumps his chest with his fist. On the heart. He's loyal. I hope so.

'Here.' I give him a five-spot. 'Do a good job and I'll give you another one.'

'Very cagey, *hombre*. OK, let's do it . . .' He pulls on a jumper that's got holes in the elbows and a woolly hat. 'Give us a cigarette.'

'Mamina lets you smoke?'

'It's nobody's fucking business but mine, *loco*,' He stares at me furiously. I've hurt his pride.

'It's just you're a bit young to be smoking, kid. You haven't even got bumfluff on your face.'

'No, it's just that you're a cheap fucker. Come on, give me a cigarette.'

'Here, take one, you little shit.' I throw the pack on the table. 'And get the fuck out of here, OK?'

'What's all the shouting about in here?' Mamina says sternly, leaning her brush against the door frame and coming inside. It drives her up the wall, people raising their voices in the house.

Quique palms the cigarette he's just nicked off me and acts all innocent.

'Nothing . . . it's just he's a bit nervous.' He pats his pockets like he's forgotten something. 'OK, Grandma, I've got to go and get Sultán. He's been tied up back at our place since Saturday. Poor little dog . . .'

He heads out and Mamina stands there looking at me.

'What's going on with you, Gringo?' she says. She's worried and it worries me. She never asks me how I am. Well, sometimes, but not often. I like it, it means she cares, but it unsettles me too.

'Nothing . . . why?' My voice quavers with anxiety. I don't know why, I feel like crying.

'You seem preoccupied. What have you got yourself mixed up in?'

'Nothing, Grandma. What makes you think I'm

mixed up in something?' I don't look at her. I pour myself another *mate*, my hand shaking. It's watery. And cold.

Mamina sighs. She sits down, puts her elbows on the table and stares at me.

'Well, be careful . . .' she says softly. 'I don't want you ending up like Antonio.'

'Like Toni? But he's a good guy, Mamina. He makes jewellery and stuff and sells it . . . I told you, I ran into him last Friday and he said to say hello.'

'I don't want to hear it. He's dead to me.' She crosses herself. 'That boy had no pity . . .'

'What happened, Mamina? For the love of God, just tell me . . .' I say worriedly. Mamina never talks in riddles. When she has something to say, she says it loud and clear.

'Same thing that will happen to you if you carry on hanging around that man who's dealing drugs in the barrio . . . I wouldn't like to have to disown you, Gringo.'

'Who are you talking about? El Jetita?'

'The very man.' Mamina stares at me. Her eyes are fierce.

She's not going to give anything else away. I know her. She goes back about her business and ignores me. What the fuck is all the mystery about?

Before I get panicky again, I go into my room.

I pick up the cardboard boxes and the blankets. The air smells heavy, an acrid smell like spunk. Just as I'm about to lie down on the bed, I notice cum stains on the sheets. That little fucking bastard . . . Quique's had a wank in my bed. I put a blanket over the stains and lie down on top of it. I take the .38 from the belt of my trousers and stuff it under the mattress where I had the whale book stashed, swap them round.

I take the money out of the book and all the money out of my pockets. I count it up. It's a small fortune. I've never seen so much cash at one time. I count it again then pocket the lot. Like Ishmael, I've got more than enough to get to hell and back. What do I do? I open the book to look for advice, to see what the guy in the book has to say, and the *loco* comes out with some shit . . .

BIRD OF ILL OMEN

Chueco comes racing down the street with the Beretta in his hand. He jerks the gat, indicating the alley leading to Oliveira's place. I don't stop to think. I walk quickly down the alley and jump the low wall, but as I'm halfway across the bag over my shoulder gets caught in my feet and I almost break my fucking neck. I push my way through the privet and hide under a kumquat tree. It's small, but dense.

Through the branches, I see Chueco fly over the garden wall, a clean jump. He looks like Superman. But he falls badly. He crashes onto the ground, almost breaking his shoulder, and rolls through the cauliflower patch. He smothers a cry and curses under his breath. He gets up, clutching his collarbone, and in the house Oliveira's dog starts barking. The guy appears at the window.

'*Você que faz aqui?! Filho da puta!*'

Chueco flashes the Beretta at him and brings a finger to his lips like he's a nurse in a hospital.

Oliveira's face changes; all the blood drains from it. Chueco waves him back inside, spinning the Beretta, not taking his finger from his lips. Oliveira closes the shutters and the dog suddenly stops barking. Chueco glances around him, confused. I give a low whistle from where I'm hiding and he comes and hunkers down with me under the tree. As soon as he's there we hear shouts from the other side of the wall. People running past.

Chueco looks me straight in the eyes. In his eyes I see fear, excitement, or the cold-blooded calm of the *merca* he's been snorting. One of them. Or all three together. We don't say a word until the shouting fades into the distance.

'They're hunting us like rats, Gringo . . .'

'Who the fuck d'you think you're telling? They came into my place. Nearly fucking capped me.'

'How many were there?'

'I don't fucking know, three, four maybe. That kid Medusa came with them so he could point me out,' I say, sparing him the details.

I must be psychic, because when I heard the kid Medusa shouting my name outside, I was stuffing the few clothes I have and the whale book into a bag. I was ready to bounce. I grabbed the strap, crawled out the bedroom window and legged it over the back wall. From the neighbour's backyard I saw a whole troop of them crashing into our place. They were all carrying. Lucky

153

Mamina had headed off to the hospital half an hour before.

Medusa stayed outside. On guard. I was about to cap the little shit, but I held back. Firing the fucking thing would only lead the bastards right to me. Like a pack of dogs. So I made a quick quiet exit the back way. Headed straight for the station. But I didn't manage to get on a train. I didn't even manage to set foot on the platform They were waiting for me. El Negrito Silva was wandering up and down the little square in front of the station. Acting the boss man. Dealing weed like nothing had happened. The place was crawling with kids from Zavaleta. Keeping watch. I recognised a couple of them. I guess they would have recognised me too. I couldn't risk waiting till El Negrito turned his back to make a run for the platform. It was too sketchy. He wasn't the only one who might see me.

'What we going to do, Gringo?' Chueco says, leaning against the tree. 'This whole thing is seriously fucked up.' His forehead's slick, a drop of sweat dances between his eyebrows. I wouldn't mind, but it's fucking cold out.

'What the fuck are you telling me for?' I say. 'Get your boss to save your scrawny arse.'

'He's a stupid fucking jerk . . . He makes out like he's this badass. Well, now he's balls-deep in shit. They're all trapped down at Fat Farías's. Anyone who shows their face gets capped.'

Chueco takes a plastic bag and a cigarette paper out of his pocket and starts skinning up a joint. His fingers are trembling. He licks the skin and finishes rolling. I spark it for him. He takes a couple of tokes and hands it to me. He blows smoke rings. He brushes the mud off his jacket and massages his shoulder through his clothes.

'You fuck up your shoulder?'

'It's nothing,' he says, playing the hard man, but I can tell it hurts.

'You eaten anything? I'm fucking starving . . .' I say, passing back the blunt. It's the middle of the afternoon and with all the shit going down I haven't had time to eat.

'We've got all the provisions we need right here, *loco*,' Chueco says, nodding to the kumquats hanging about a foot above our heads.

I reach up, pick a fistful and eat them one after the other, stuffing them into my mouth. They're bitter. I pull a face, like when I was a kid.

Chueco tries one and does the same. I laugh to myself. We're like a couple of kids hiding when they're in trouble. Trying to postpone the beating *papá*'s going to give us. But sooner or later we're going to have to come out. Hiding from him just makes the *hijo de puta* with the belt angrier. I never knew my old man. Neither did Chueco. But I still feel like a furious father is waiting out there ready to make us toe the line. Actually, we might have been better off if some drunken fuck of a father had knocked out our baby teeth. Might have saved us from what's waiting out there now. The barrio, hunger, fate, fear . . . We're the sons of one or other of the bastards out there. And it doesn't matter. They're all vicious.

While I'm thinking about this shit, Chueco has been bogarting the spliff. I grab it off him and smoke it down till it burns my fingers.

'So? What do we do?' he says, eyes bulging out of his head.

'Get out of here?'

'No fucking way I'm moving from here until after it gets dark —'

Chueco suddenly shuts up and pricks up his ears.

'Listen,' he whispers. 'Listen.'

Gunshots. And they're coming from somewhere close by. Fat Farías's place probably. As I was sneaking away from the station, I could feel it was all going to go off. They've spent most of the day amassing ammunition. Now it's all-out war. And it won't be over until they've sorted out their turf once and for all.

'Why are they going to all this trouble to cap a couple of nobodies like us?' I say, thinking aloud. 'You want to tell me?'

'Because we're the ones who started this when we fucked over those kids and took their stash.

Because it's a lot easier to cap us than to take down one of El Jetita's men and it sends out the same message. It tells everyone Charly's not gonna be fucked with.' Chueco rattles off the explanation in one sentence until he runs out of breath. He's speeding.

Huddled under the tree, my legs are starting to cramp. I want to get out of here. I get to my feet and try to straighten up between the branches. I manage more or less and then, in the distance, I hear the call of a non-existent bird. Almost like the way I do it, but different. This bird is hoarse and angry. Whoever's whistling is blowing too hard, wasting air squawking so loudly. It's Quique. He's trying to find me without giving the game away. He's finally fucking learned to whistle through his thumbs. All the times he tried and couldn't do it . . . Beggars can't be choosers. Needs must . . . All that shit.

I answer. Cupping my hands and blowing softly between my thumbs, fluttering the fingers of my right hand. I do it very carefully so the bird call sounds real. I'm not going to be the one that gets us discovered. I sit down again, cross my legs and wait. Chueco looks at me. He doesn't understand. I don't say anything. I wait for an answer. It comes about two or three minutes later. Closer this time. I call again and wait for a reply. Chueco raises his eyebrows questioningly. I whistle a couple more times until the croaking bird is right on top of us. Just the other side of the wall.

Slowly, carefully, I pop my head over the garden wall but I can't see Quique anywhere. I hear a noise behind me. I turn and see Sultán coming through the privet and, behind him, Quique's head wriggling through a hole in the wire fence like a weasel. I signal him over to the kumquat tree. Sultán sniffs the hiding place suspiciously before padding inside, Quique pushing him because he's blocking his way.

'So, what's the story, kid?'

'They're combing the whole barrio . . . They're looking for you guys, aren't they?' he says to me, untangling a branch that's caught in his hair.

'Thanks for the newsflash, kid,' I interrupt him. 'Tell me something I don't know.'

'This dog is fucking retarded,' Chueco says, backing away from Sultán.

Quique heroically ignores him and looks at me again.

'What d'you want me to say? There's more of them than flies on shit, they're crawling all over the place. Remember when El Sapo Medina smacked that young cop down by the station, and the whole fucking force came out looking for him? Well, this is way worse. These guys are much better organised and they're seriously carrying.'

'What do we do, Gringo?' Chueco says. 'This is turning to shit –'

'Hang on, let me think for a second.' I shut him up.

I spark up a cigarette. Chueco immediately holds out his hand for one. I give him the pack, but his hands are shaking so much he can't get the cigarette out.

'What's the matter, gunslinger?' I take it out for him and give him a light. He's a mess.

'What if we hole up with my people for a couple of days?' he stammers, sucking on the cigarette with all his lungs.

I tell him no. I glance at Quique, who shakes his head and blinks slowly.

'What?'

'They've already been round your squat,' Quique says. 'Broke old man Soria's nose. And that posh guy, what's his name? Willi? They nearly fucking ended him. Beat the living shit out of him. The guy couldn't speak. They thought he was holding out on them, so then they really laid into him.'

'How d'you know all this?'

'Because I saw them, Gringo. I'm telling you, these guys are fucked up. They even stopped that arsehole Santi in the street and put a gun in his mouth. Dumb fuck shat his pants. Told them he didn't know where you guys were, that if he did, he'd tell them everything.'

'They been round mine?' I ask, thinking about Mamina. If they've touched her, I'll fucking die.

'They went in the back way, posted a lookout, smashed the place up,' Quique says, and from the look on my face, he can already tell what I'm thinking. 'Don't worry about your grandma. She's staying over at the hospital tonight to keep my *mamá* company. And if she comes back in the morning and this shit's still going down, I'll stop her.'

Chueco's eyes are popping out of his head. Quique pokes at the ground with a stick. We say nothing for a bit, but my brain's working overtime. Quique sighs and looks at me. What I see in his eyes isn't worry or fear, it's sadness.

'This is going to end badly, Gringo,' he says. 'Take my word for it –'

'You're the one who's going to end, you little shit,' Chueco roars. 'You and your predictions, fucking bird of ill omen.'

Sultán pricks up his ears. Sniffs the air. He's sensed something. Inside the house Oliveira's dog senses it too and starts yapping. Sultán barks back.

'Quiet, Sultán,' Quique whispers and slaps the dog's nose.

'Take a hike, will you, and take your fucking dog with you before you fuck everything up.'

'Chill, *loco*,' Quique says. 'Stop stressing.'

This only makes Chueco worse.

'Go on, Quique,' I say softly as Chueco is still fuming and cursing. 'Take the dog and go. But stay close, and when you see the coast is clear, give me a whistle.'

He nods and looks greedily at the cigarette I'm raising to my lips. He pats Sultán's flank and gets to his feet.

'Quique.' I call him back.

'What?' He half turns.

'Take care, yeah?' I say and offer him a cigarette.

'You too, Gringo.'

THE SIEGE

As I drop onto the roof of Fat Farías's place, I hear
the first gunshot. I duck automatically and as I turn I
see Chueco standing there like a pillar of fucking salt
on the neighbouring roof. He's bricking it so bad he
can't move. More gunshots. And people inside the
bar start returning fire.

'Jesus, move it. You looking to get killed?'

Chueco takes a step back then jumps. We slink
along the corrugated-iron roof like weasels. Bullets
whining just above our heads like a swarm of
angry wasps. I didn't expect it to sound like this.
It's enough to make you piss yourself. When we
get to the back of the roof, I grip the gutter with
one hand, swing my torso down, and thump three
times on the kitchen door. The answer is a
shotgun blast that rips past my face leaving the
metal door looking like a sieve.

'Don't fucking shoot,' Chueco yells. 'It's us!'

Though my mouth desperately opens and closes,

not a sound comes out. My heart stopped when the gun went off. My turn to play statues now. Inside, someone shouts something I can't make out and the door is kicked open. Chueco scrambles over me, drops from the roof, using the force of his fall to wing into the kitchen. I turn myself round so as not to drop head first and follow him. A fat guy with a sawn-off Itaca slams the door shut as soon as I'm inside and leans his back against the wall. For protection. I stand there, staring at him, hypnotised by his huge grey moustache. It looks like a dead rat. The fat fucker stares back at me hard.

'Hey, guys, the cavalry's arrived! We're saved!' El Jetita shouts from the far side of the kitchen, gun in one hand and a police radio in the other.

It takes me a second before I notice that, between El Jetita and where we're standing by the back door, there's a ton of people. The narrow kitchen looks like the carriage of a train at rush hour. A night train speeding through the darkness. Pitch dark, no moon. Heading straight off a cliff. This much I can tell from the looks of uncertainty and panic on the faces of the passengers. Riquelme, the old whore, is standing next to me sobbing, her whole face distorted so her wrinkles look like furrows of despair. Rubén is scratching his ear with the double barrel of a shotgun and chain-smoking. Eyes wide open but vacant. Staring at some fixed point.

Yanina is sitting on the kitchen counter. She looks like she's about to cry. Her eyes meet mine. Her chin quivers. She clutches her old man's shoulder tightly, hanging limply against him like a rag doll. With his turban of bandages, his dislocated jaw and his empty eyes, Fat Farías looks like a ghost.

Next to him, El Negro Sosa is necking a bottle of gin, his frown screwed up tighter than a fist. A semi-automatic dangles from his right hand. His shirt is spattered with blood.

Pampita looks up at me pitifully from the floor, pleading with me for I don't know what, but I do know that whatever it is I can't give it to her. She's calm. Not crying. Barefoot. Wearing a sort of shabby, tattered dressing gown. With one hand she cradles the head of the skinny guy, Fabián, using the other to press a crude improvised bandage against his chest. The spreading red stain of the wound is screaming for someone to take him to hospital. Lying in a pool of blood, Fabián gasps, his face twitching like he's got a nervous tic. I don't know shit about anatomy, but from the site of the bullet wound, I figure it hit his liver.

There are no windows in the kitchen. It's just a built-in unit at the back of the bar. It's the best place to hold out against the siege. But it's a breeding ground for fear. Panic pervades the room, bouncing blindly off the walls, ricocheting inside

164

our heads. We're all aboard a night train, and the most dangerous passenger is fear. If the train goes off the rails, fear will be to blame. Simple as. Because it's fear that's laying siege.

'Come on, *señoritas*, I want all of you out front. The only girls I want to see in this kitchen are the ones wearing skirts,' roars El Jetita. He's playing the General. He's taking command until the invisible passenger does for him too. And he carries on. Faster and faster. There's nothing else to do. 'Hey, Robledo,' he says to the fat guy with the sawn-off Itaca, 'stay here and guard the back in case they send round a kamikaze. And Farías, dig something out of the fridges so the women can make us something to eat. This isn't going to be over any time soon . . . You got any bread left?'

Fat Farías nods. He's so fucking scared he can't speak. But Yanina won't let go of him. And Farías doesn't move until El Jetita roars, 'Move it, *che*, don't just fucking stand there. And that goes for the rest of you, move it, come on . . .' He grabs Chueco by the back of the neck and pushes him, which gets the crowd moving.

On his way out, El Negro Sosa slips him the bottle of gin and whispers something in his ear.

'Hey, Sapito, how's it looking?' shouts El Jetita as he walks through the strip curtain.

'All quiet for the minute . . .'

As I step into the front of the bar, I see him. I

see him in the orange haze from the street lights, because the bar itself is in darkness. And a complete fucking mess. It's El Sapo Medina's kid brother. He's posted by the window at the front. He's got his long hair in a ponytail and he's wearing a baseball cap turned backwards. He doesn't take his eyes off the street. The kid watches too many movies. Thinks he's a fucking sniper. Though I have to admit he's got the gear for it. The barrel of his rifle is resting in the small gap between the window ledge and the metal shutters, which have been pulled down. The windows have been shot to shit. A couple of the Formica tables have been blasted away too, and the football photos from the Copa Libertadores which Fat Farías had hanging on the walls. There's glass everywhere.

The gun he's using is a FAL. Least I'm guessing it is, I haven't actually seen one before. The question is where the fuck he got his hands on a piece of kit like that. Far as I was aware, Sapo's kid brother spent all day every day hanging out with Santi. They're both nuts about racing and cars. And he always seemed like a sweet kid. Now it turns out he's one of El Jetita's soldiers. And he's handling heavy artillery. I clearly don't understand a fucking thing.

The police radio squawks and crackles. El Jetita puts it to his ear. Just for the fuck of it, because it looks cool. Over the static I can hear a nasal voice asking for a unit to be sent to the junction by the refinery. The cop taking the call uses all the codes and shit. This is on the Feds' open band.

'So what are we going to do with Fabián?' Rubén says to El Jetita passing him the gin. 'Guess he's going to croak, huh?'

'You're saying he can't hold out?' El Negro Sosa butts in.

Rubén clicks his tongue and says impatiently, 'Hold out? Have you seen the fucking state of him?'

'He's going to have to hold on as best he can, *viejo*,' El Jetita cuts him off. 'Stay cool and calm like Gardel on that plane. What the fuck else can we do?'

Just then, three gunshots come through the side window. One hits the bar, the other two rip through the walls. Everyone hits the floor.

'Sapito, you little fucker, you're supposed to be keeping lookout,' El Jetita screams at him.

'What can I do if they don't show their arses?' Sapo's kid brother yells back, blindly firing in bursts.

'If you can't see them what the fuck are you doing wasting ammo? Jesus fucking Christ, how the fuck am I supposed to handle this with a bunch of kids?' El Jetita rants. He says something I don't hear to El Negro Sosa then starts shouting again. 'Chueco, over here. And you, Gringo, the other side! Anything that moves, I want you to fill it with lead! Doesn't matter if it's a stray dog, a gust of wind or your fucking mother. Same goes for you, Sapito! Is that clear! Move it, *loco*, come on!'

Chueco starts crawling across the broken glass between the upturned chairs and tables. I push the bag that's still slung over my shoulder behind my back and crawl after him. Then I feel someone grab me by the ankle. I turn my head and El Jetita, looking scared, whispers, 'If we can't sort this thing, Gringo, you're going to help me out. You're going to get Toni to come and negotiate.'

'Sure, maybe I can let you have my sister too. Pity I haven't got one. Who the fuck do you take me for?!'

I don't say it, but that's what I'm thinking, and from the look on my face he has to know. But I'm also thinking other stuff, like what the fuck has Toni got to do with this shit? He's been gone from the barrio for ages . . .

'You heard me,' El Jetita says, seeing the expression on my face. 'And don't try anything smart or I'll fucking end you. Now go on, get moving.'

Chueco is already posted on one side of the front window, back to the wall, legs apart. He's propped up on his left elbow so he can turn easily and he's peering through the crack under the security shutter. What few rays of daylight are left slip between the frame and the metal shutter which hasn't been rolled down completely. It's through this gap he aims the Beretta. And through this gap that night seeps in. A damp cool breeze. The last three shots added a new constellation to the holes in the shutter. Street light glimmers through them. Like stars against a black sky.

I crawl to the other side, take out the .38, pull the bag off my shoulder and sit on it. I watch through the crack, but nothing. The street is deserted. I look carefully to see if I can see where the shots came from. The corner, the building site across the street, the patch of waste ground further off, the roofs . . . But there's nothing. We're surrounded by ghosts. Or brothers of the invisible passenger.

Chueco's eyes scream despair. His eyebrows collect the sweat from his forehead. They're dripping. Like he's just played a five-a-side match. The passenger's got him by the balls. And it's not about to let go. It's obvious. He's about to say something to me but I signal for him to wait. To listen.

El Jetita's police radio is still chirruping and giving off static. He's behind the bar with Rubén and El Negro Sosa. They're talking. But from where I am I can't hear what they're saying. What

I can hear loud and clear is El Jetita barking into the radio.

'Commissioner Zanetti, do you copy me? Come in, over.'

He repeats the call over and over until the radio finally crackles into life and spits, 'Zanetti here. I copy you. Who is this? Over.'

'About fucking time!' El Jetita says before pressing the button on the radio. 'Commissioner, it's Ricardo. Been trying to reach you all afternoon. We've got a serious problem here. Over.'

It's the first time I've ever heard El Jetita's name. His real name, the one behind the alias. And it's the first time I've ever heard El Jetita use this tone of voice. Meek, imploring.

'Yeah . . . an officer told me some fool was trying to get me on the radio but wouldn't give a name. You know you're not supposed to use this frequency. Just this once, I'm breaking the rules for you. What do you want, sweetie? I don't have time to waste. Over.'

'Commissioner, one of my boys has been shot and unless he gets medical attention, he's not going to make it. I need you to clear up the situation, because right now they've got us trapped inside Farías's bar . . . Over.'

'What are you coming crying to me for, Ricardito? What am I, your *mamá*? I thought we agreed. You sort the turf out with Charly; when that's done you and I can do a deal. Don't bust my balls, sweetie, I've got enough shit on my plate right now with the strikers and picketers down on Zavaleta Bridge and I've got to be up first thing tomorrow to deal with the teachers' demonstration. Over.'

'I'm calling because Robledo who's down here with me says he saw two officers out there with the guys who've got us trapped.' El Jetita's still calm, but now he's a little gruff. 'What the hell's going on, Zanetti? Come in. Over.'

'Listen. Robledo's not on the force any more, and I don't trust anything he says. So just sort out your own business and don't come telling tales to me. Oh, and one more thing . . . Remember what I told you last time. Don't leave a bunch of gunshot stiffs lying around the place. If you give me grief or create extra work for me, the deal's off, OK? Right . . . I've got to go . . . work.' The radio gives a last belch of static and then goes silent.

'Fuck you, Zanetti, fucking *hijo de puta!*' Rubén explodes. 'I'm going to make you pay for this, and pay good!'

El Jetita joins in the litany of abuse. El Negro Sosa says something too, but I don't hear it.

All through this conversation, Chueco hasn't taken his eyes off me. Now he raises his eyebrows and whispers, 'What the fuck have we got ourselves into, Gringo?'

171

'What choice did we have? This is a war. If we'd stayed out there, we'd be dead . . .'

'And we won't be in this rathole?' he hisses.

'We'll see,' I say without much conviction.

Chueco groans, wipes his forehead with the back of his hand, bends down a little so he can scan the street. We stay like that in silence for a couple of minutes until, without looking at me, he says quietly, 'Gringo, you have to believe me, I've always been straight with you . . . Only reason I didn't tell you that the bust on Farías's place was a set-up was so you wouldn't bail. And then after that thing with Santi, you just ended up believing what you wanted to believe . . . I wasn't dealing dope, I was just getting rid of a couple of lumps of hash I nicked from El Jetita, that's all, I swear.

'We're cool, Chueco. Jesus, what's with you? You getting sentimental?'

'I'm just saying . . .'

'Chill, it's all good,' I say, and I feel a lump in my throat.

THE LOOKOUT CHEATS

I cheat. I start skipping pages, two at a time, then three at a time. And it still seems like the story's not getting anywhere. Or if it is, it's moving fucking slowly. Barely crawling along. Hesitant, groping its way. This bastard Ishmael goes on too much. He goes into every detail. From the shape of a whale's jawbone to the way the crews on whaling boats party when they meet up out at sea. Sometimes it's slower than swimming through snot.

All I wanted was to sail off into the sunset on Captain Ahab's ship, but the speed the *Pequod* moves is a joke. A piss-poor joke. It's like it's sailing in slow motion. Even the minute hand is moving faster. Which is saying something, because ever since we've been trapped here, time's been stretching like chewing gum. Last time I asked El Sapito Medina, it was half three. And that was a long time ago. But it doesn't look like it's going to start getting light any time soon.

El Sapito's obviously bored playing the sniper. He's propped the FAL against the shutter. Inoffensive. Right now he's nodding off with his baseball cap pulled down over his eyes. Chueco too. Dozing off then jolting awake. Every now and then he opens his eyes and gives me this strange, confused look. Like he's woken up without knowing where he is or what the fuck is happening. I keep reading. I struggle against tiredness, against fear. I ward off fear as best I can by reading the whale book, but Ishmael's not making it easy for me. Nothing's happening. Nothing's happening outside either.

So I go on reading. I tilt the book towards the window so I can make the most of a beam of light from the street outside that filters through a hole in the shutter. I use the hole to scan the night and I skim through the pages. But nothing changes. Day refuses to break. And in the book it's worse.

There's no sign of life from El Jetita, Rubén or El Negro Sosa. For a while there, they were holed up behind the counter playing *truco*, calling out bids like every hand was life or death. But their fondness for pills and gin moved on to class As. With every hand their nostrils blared like trumpets.

'Stingy fuckers don't even pass it round,' Chueco whispered, half dead with fear. Now he's asleep, his worried little face like a kid having a nightmare. Breaks your heart just to look at him.

The three chiefs have probably fallen asleep over their cards by now. It's the only thing that would explain the quiet. Unless they're playing some card game for deaf mutes. Which I doubt. I'd be happy if they'd been snorting *paco* cut with naphthalene. Or better still, caustic soda.

What really scares me now is the silence from the kitchen. And not because of Yani, though I feel bad for her. I can hardly bring myself to look her in the eye now. And it's not for Pampita, however much I feel sorry for her. Or for old Riquelme or Fat Farías. And no way is it for Robledo, the fucking *milico* turncoat . . .

No, the silence that's freaking me out is the other guy. The skinny guy, Fabián. That kid's down to the last cigarette in the pack. And I'm freaked out because I've got a feeling everyone in there is asleep except him. I feel like he's keeping me company. As though we're keeping watch together tonight. I'm waiting for the first streak of dawn in the sky. Fabián is ringing down the curtain once and for all. Turning off the lights and closing up. Dawn or no dawn. That's why he's not sleeping. Either that or he's already woken up somewhere far from this nightmare. Although he may be wincing with pain, squeezing his eyes tight shut with every twinge, right now his eyes are wide open. I'd swear it. Open and staring out at the night.

Just like Ishmael when it's his turn to go up into the crow's nest. To climb up into the barrel on the masthead to watch for the spouts of distant whales. Since Ahab can recognise the spout of the white whale, he forces his crew to stand watch twenty-four hours a day. Ishmael takes the night watch. The silvery jet of water appears and disappears in the moonlight like a phantom. They follow it for a couple of days, but it doesn't reappear. Ishmael tells the men it's a waste of time since what they're hunting is not Moby Dick, but Ahab's doom. He's a smart-arse. All the way through the book it's like he's waiting for something bad to happen, like he can tell the future. But he's cheating. Because he already knows what's going to happen. The story he's telling happened years ago. And he came through it. That's the only reason why he can tell the story. He already knows what's going to happen. I don't. Neither does Fabián, but he can imagine.

The gold doubloon is still there, nailed to the mast, waiting for someone to say they've spotted Moby Dick on the horizon. But it never happens. The days go by, and old Ahab gets crazier and crazier. The first thing he does whenever they encounter another ship is ask the captain for news of Moby Dick. And they keep going, following the trail. People die along the way. Drown. Harpoon boats are sunk. But the hunt never ends. They sail almost all the way to Japan. And just when it seems like they're going to find him any moment now, old Ahab breaks his whalebone leg. The ship's carpenter has to make him a new one from the keel of one of the harpoon boats that was smashed.

The carpenter's a weird character. And he appears out of nowhere in the middle of the book. He's an old labourer who put out to sea because his whole family is dead. The guy's got nothing to lose.

Suddenly, the story speeds up and lots of things start happening. Now I can't cheat any more. Ishmael won't let me. Won't let me skip a single page. Things are getting worse and worse. Overnight, Ishmael's little friend, the harpooner with all the tattoos, gets sick. He thinks he's going to die. He gets the carpenter to measure him and make a coffin. He climbs into it with his harpoon, his idol and a bunch of junk he wants to take with him into the afterlife. Then, when Ishmael's already bawling about him dying, the guy says he's not ready to die yet and climbs out again. The 'savage' gets better just like that, because he wills it. But that's not the half of it. It's not over yet.

Since the coffin is about as useful as ears on a deaf guy, they decide to use it as a lifeboat, because they lost the one they had when some guy drowned. Now Ishmael really starts being a smart-arse. Now I really want to beat the shit out of him. He must think we're all a bunch of retards. What's he doing coming up with all this bullshit? OK, so the coffin's made of wood and I guess wood floats, but it's a bit of a stretch from that to deciding to use it as a lifeboat. Either you're a stupid fuck or you already know how everything turns out. The only person who could use a lifeboat like that is Fabián.

A DROP OF WATER

I keep on reading. The old carpenter is called Perth.
And he's not just a carpenter, he works with metal
too. Ahab gives him his best knives and asks him
to make a harpoon. It has to be good steel if it's
going to pierce Moby Dick's heart. So Perth forges
the harpoon and old Ahab wants to christen it
with the blood of the harpooners. Because they're
pagans, according to him. One of them is Queequeg,
Ishmael's cannibal friend who was about to die a
couple of chapters ago. Then there's this tall black
guy and the third is an American Indian. Ahab
mixes some blood from all three and, as he dips the
point of the harpoon into it, he swears an oath. Like
it's a fucking macumba ritual. I can almost hear the
whistle of the red-hot metal as it's dipped into the
blood. But I look up from the book and I hear the
whistle again. It's coming from outside.

A burst of gunfire drowns out everything.
Suspended time explodes in a symphony of

gunshots. Fear speeds up my reactions. I'm already firing back.

'Wha . . . ?' Chueco jerks awake and starts firing.

El Sapito's FAL spits bullets. The metal shutter shudders like a drumskin. Bullets still zip through the metal, taking chips out of tables and chunks of plaster from the walls.

'Jesus fuck!' someone shouts from behind the counter. El Jetita or Rubén, I'm not sure which.

I want to peek through the crack, but I don't dare. The shutter is shaking hard now. If I show my face, I'm going to get it shot off. I can feel it in the trembling in my legs, the chill running up my spine. I fire blindly, not even bothering to try to aim.

I turn and see Rubén, lying on his stomach, slithering quickly towards the door, pushing the shotgun in front of him. He looks like a snake. A fat snake. He pushes the door open a crack with the barrel of the shotgun, and fires off rounds of pellets from ground level.

I'm still firing but the trigger just clicks dully. The cylinder's empty. Chueco glances over at me and, still firing, rummages in his jacket pocket, fishes out a box of .38 shells and tosses it to me. As I'm reloading, I hear the same whistle I heard before the firing started. But this time, it goes on and on, panicked, hysterical. I know it's Quique, and I feel a knot in my stomach.

El Jetita shouts an order I don't hear. There's a silence. I put one eye to the crack. My left eye. There's a dark shape lying in the middle of the road in a pool of blood that keeps spreading. It's got too much hair to be a kid. It's a dog. I'm sure it's Sultán. That's why Quique was whistling so desperately.

Above a half-built wall in the construction site opposite, I see a gun appear. Then a head slowly follows it. But before I can even see the eyebrows, there's a bang and it disappears suddenly. Where the head was, there's now a gaping hole in the wall and a cloud of dust from the shotgun blast.

'See? That's how it's done,' Rubén yells, ecstatic. 'Come on, guys, shoot the fuckers! What are you waiting for?'

One down. But the firestorm starts up again. The shutter looks like it's about to cave in any minute now. El Sapito is still shooting in regular bursts, but it doesn't seem to be scaring them off. On the contrary, it feels like there's more of them. Sultán's blood glistens red now and the street is glowing yellow. When did dawn break? All that waiting for daybreak only for it to happen without warning, the moment snatched away by the rush of adrenalin and the smell of gunpowder.

There's no sign of the gunfire stopping, but after a while there's a pause between the bursts. Chueco is pale, but he seems calm. He gives me a quick look out of the corner of his eye. I don't know what to make of the gesture.

'Gringo!' El Jetita shouts. 'Over here!' He signals for me to head for the kitchen.

El Negro Sosa clears the counter in a single jump and in two steps he's standing next to me. He's come to take my place. He shakes me by the shoulder like he's trying to wake me. I don't know what the fuck he's doing it for, since I'm not asleep. Or not as much as I'd like to be.

'Come on, move your arse!' he says. 'Leave them to me.'

I grab the bag and the whale book lying on the ground, stuff the book into the bag and sling it over my shoulder. I make to stand up, but another bullet rips through the shutter and makes me change my mind. Better to crawl over.

'And where the fuck d'you think you're going, *loco*?'

'I'm going with him,' Chueco says curtly.

'Stay where you are,' El Negro snaps. 'What are you, his boyfriend? You afraid someone's going to bust your girlfriend's arse?'

'You fucking deaf? Where Gringo goes, I go,' Chueco says in a tone that leaves no room for discussion.

'Little shit! You think you're a big man? I'll fucking carve you up!'

'Hey, girls, don't start,' El Jetita says to smooth

things over. 'Leave him, Negro. If he wants to risk his neck, let him. The kid knows what he's doing.'

El Negro Sosa flips him the finger. Chueco doesn't react.

I crawl into the kitchen and stand up again. Chueco follows me. El Jetita's blocking my way. And my line of sight.

'Hey, Robledo, how are things?'

'It's all fine,' says the *milico*. 'Been a bit calmer back here since Fabián –'

'What? He snuffed it?'

'Couple of hours ago. He's cold as a nun's cunt now.'

'Jesus Christ! That's all I fucking need,' says El Jetita. 'The straw that breaks the camel's back.' He walks across to the filthy mattress. There's someone sleeping on it right next to the corpse.

Fabián is whiter than a sheet of paper. His mouth is hanging open. Someone's closed his eyes. Old Riquelme is sitting on a beer crate next to him, face like stone, watching over him. On the other side is Pampita. Sitting on the ground. Her face even more blank.

Fat Farías stops El Jetita and pulls him to one side with his good hand – he's still got his right hand in the dirty sling, but the bandage turban on his head is gone.

'Ricardo, we need to talk,' he says. 'This whole

thing has got out of hand.' He's serious. He's using up his last cartridge of dignity.

'Don't bust my balls, Gordo, can't you see this isn't the right time?' El Jetita cuts him dead, shaking Farías off him like he's a street kid begging for change.

Meanwhile, I go over to Yanina who's still on the counter, curled into a ball, her back pressed against the wall. Her hair falls over her eyes, her face is turned inward. She's looking at me but she doesn't see me. I whisper in her ear, tell her to wait for me, tell her that when I come back the two of us are getting out of here. But she doesn't react. I feel like I'm whispering to a wax dummy.

'The guys are going to go out the back way,' El Jetita explains to Robledo. Then, turning to us, he says to me, 'Griguito, you're going to go out there and send Toni in to me. Tell him to fire three shots in the air and wave a white flag – we'll let him in. And tell him not to try anything, OK? Tell him to come in unarmed, tell him I won't be carrying either. We'll sit down and hammer out a deal everyone can live with and that'll be the end of it. You got that?'

'Who told you Toni's out there?' I say.

'It's . . . I know him. If he's not there, he'll be here any minute now. Charly will have called him as soon as he pulled this shit . . . Me and those two fuckers go way back, I know them . . . But why the fuck am I explaining this shit to you? Just do what you're told, kid, and shut your hole!'

'And what makes you think I'm going to offer him to you on a plate? I walk out that door, you'll never fucking set eyes on me again.' I regret the words before I've even said them.

El Jetita gives a roar of laughter and stares at me. He twists the knife wound he's got for a mouth, and time seems to stand still. I know this look all too well.

'You've got a pair of balls on you, Gringo, I'll give you that. You'll go far.' He gives me a wink.

He raises a hand as though to pat me on the shoulder, and before I've got time to react, he grabs me by the throat, slams my head against the wall and drags me back. Robledo steps aside and El Jetita's hand squeezes harder. He's choking me. El Jetita pulls me towards him until his lips brush against my ear. This leaves me facing Chueco. He blinks slowly and shakes his head. Almost imperceptibly, but I see it. If this was a game of *truco* and we were partnered, he'd be telling me he doesn't have the cards to win this hand.

'Now listen up and listen good,' El Jetita whispers, and what has me shitting my pants is the calm relaxed tone of his voice as he strangles me. 'There's three reasons you're going to do exactly what I tell you. First, if you don't, I'll hunt you down wherever you're hiding and I'll gouge your eyes out. With my bare hands. Got it? Second, because I'm guessing you want to pay Toni back for what he did to Deep Throat. I mean, she was your *mamá*, wasn't she? And third, you'll do it for the kid. Pretty little thing, Yani, isn't she? You fancy her, don't you? Good. Well, if you don't do your homework like a good boy, I'll make it my business to fuck her up. She'll be spread like a tango dancer's legs on a Saturday night. You won't even be able to jerk off thinking about her again . . . Am I clear?'

He relaxes his grip and I breathe. I can feel my legs buckle. El Jetita gives Robledo a signal and the Fed opens the back door.

'Now get the fuck out of here,' El Jetita says and slaps me upside the head. 'You too, move it . . .' he says to Chueco.

We go out and Robledo closes the door behind us. We stand there, hidden behind the pile of beer crates. Undecided. I'm still coughing and spitting. I get my breath back. Chueco doesn't open his mouth. I look at him and jerk my head towards the roof. He clicks his tongue, so I don't push it. I'm not exactly thrilled at the idea of having to crawl across the roofs again. We'd be like ducks at a fairground up there. Easy targets. Chueco jerks the Beretta towards the low wall next to the little corrugated-iron storage shed.

'Let's do it,' I say. I don't stop to think, because if I do, I'll never move.

Having just drawn the .38 for no reason, I stuff it in my belt, put both hands on the top of the wall and vault it. Before I've even hit the ground, I hear two shots. They've clocked us. Hunkered on the ground, I count the seconds. Four, five, six . . . Chueco lands next to me and there's another burst of gunfire. In a couple of seconds they'll be right on top of us. There's no lock on the gate. I slam the bolt back, but the gate won't open. Chueco grabs my shoulder. I turn and he jerks his thumb to say he'll go first. He's decided.

He manages to get the gate open, fires out at random and legs it. I follow, firing the .38, trying to aim at something, but I can't see anything. Bullets whistle past us. Another swarm of angry wasps . . . and Chueco drops like a sack of potatoes. I need to drag him along with me. Because now I can see two figures at the corner, the dawn light framing them from behind. I aim and fire, one, two, three shots. I hear a scream and they disappear. I figure I must have hit one of them. I haul Chueco to his feet by his armpits and he lets out a hoarse moan like he's being split in two.

'Come on, come on . . . Move it, Chueco, don't fucking bail on me now!' I scream, dragging him behind me like he's drunk.

We stumble across the road.

'Go on, *loco*, move it!'

But Chueco slumps against me. He's not breathing, he's making gurgling noises, choking and spitting. They shot him up good. Everything's going to shit. A long shadow appears at the corner and starts firing. Chueco's head lurches and rolls until he leans it on my shoulder. His legs aren't working. They're like putty.

'Stop, Gringo, stop, leave me here . . .' he says and pukes up blood. A lot of blood. I feel it trickle down my side. I'm losing him. He slumps to the ground. I manage to drag him into a doorway and hammer furiously on the door, hoping for a miracle. I've completely lost it.

'Open up! For fuck's sake, open the fucking door!'

'It's too late, Gringo, leave it,' he says haltingly, choking on red puke. 'Just get out of here.'

'Come on, *loco*, hang in there!' I yell, but my voice breaks. 'Hang in there just for a bit. I'll go get Santi and we'll take you to hospital . . .' I say, loading the .38.

I try to do it quickly, but I can't. It's not that my hands are shaking, the whole world is shaking. The gun is shaking and the bullets jump out of my hands. The air is moving, the street is swaying. Chueco's eyelids are trembling like the early dawn light, trembling like a drop of water suspended on a thread. The way a droplet hesitates just before it falls. I manage to get the bullets into the chamber, but the drop falls. And I run. Run before the droplet hits the ground. Run as I hear the wasps swarm all around me.

MESSAGES

The giant reeds scratch my hands, my face, rip
my clothes to shreds, but I can't sit still. I can
hear a voice talking to me. Sending me conflicting
messages. It whimpers, swears, launches into some
long-winded speech until it chokes, whispers, sobs.
It's following close behind and I can't seem to shake
it. I peer through the reeds looking for the source,
but all I can see are rats. The rats that nest in the
rubbish tip on the riverbank. They shriek as I get
close and disappear.

I haven't got a hanky so I blow my nose into my
T-shirt. It's like cardboard. The blood Chueco
puked up over me has dried. I peel off the T-shirt,
go down to the water and wash myself. The river
is black, stagnant and stinks of rotting garbage, but
I still wash myself in it. I stink of something far
worse. The smell of fear.

I take the clean T-shirt stashed in my bag and
pull it on. My trousers are stained too and they're

ripped at the knee, but I keep them on. They're the only pair I have. And it's cold. I put on my windcheater again even though it itches like fuck. The nylon keeps getting snagged on things as I make my way through the scrubland.

As I blow through my thumbs, whistling to Quique, the voice fades. The arsehole who's been tormenting me finally shuts up. Cupping my hands, I whistle again and it's only then that I realise I've been talking to myself all fucking morning. It's enough to drive me insane.

I need to get a grip. I go back to the reeds, find a little clearing and try to sleep for a bit. Rats are the least of my worries. What's inside my head is much more dangerous. I can't really switch my brain off completely, but at least I manage to rest. After a while, I feel much better. I keep whistling every now and then, though it's probably pointless. Doesn't matter how loud Quique makes the non-existent bird call, I'm never going to hear him if he's on the other side of the barrio. But I don't give up hope, I keep whistling.

As the sun reaches its height, the sky clouds over. And I start to feel thirsty. I don't feel hungry at all. It doesn't feel like I have a stomach any more, I lost it while I was running. Instead I feel a gaping hole there. A storm drain swallowing up my twisted insides.

An animal barks in answer to my bird call and I

go quiet. I hear the lazy squeak of a wheel axle. I pull my gun and, through the reeds, I can make out the scrawny dog snuffling around close to me. A cart slowly rumbles past. I recognise it from the half-dead nag pulling it. It gets turned out to graze on the waste ground by the station. I've seen it a couple of times. I've never seen the bearded guy holding the reins before, though. The dog trots along behind the cart. And the squeak of the wheels gradually fades as the cart heads for the rubbish tip. The guy's a *cartonero* – picks through rubbish for cans, paper, bottles, anything worth anything. A long hard slog, sifting through garbage. Today's no different as far as he's concerned. Doesn't matter to him that there's guys firing guns a couple of blocks away. He's got a day's work to do. It's just another day for him. Not for me.

I can still hear the squeak of the axle in the distance and the sound soothes me a bit. When it finally fades, I start up with the bird calls again. After a while, I think I hear the same call answering me, but from another dimension. I don't know if maybe what I'm hearing is just an echo, but I keep on whistling. And gradually, the other person takes shape. Comes closer. He's followed the whistle all the way through the barrio. This last stretch is the hardest. Quique's trying to work out exactly where the call is coming from. A couple more bird calls and he gets to the cart tracks. I pop my head above the reeds so he can see me. He makes like he's leaving so as to throw anyone who's watching off the scent and ducks into the reeds.

'They killed my dog, Gringo,' he says, his voice quavering.

'They capped Chueco,' I say, my voice trembling like his.

He doesn't say anything. He comes over, hugs me and pats me on the back. Like we haven't clapped eyes on each other for fucking years. I feel embarrassed. I feel my face crumple like I'm about to cry, but I don't want him to see me go to pieces. I hug him hard then quickly light a cigarette. I give him one.

Quique smokes it slowly, staring at the ground. A rotting carpet of leaves, twigs and garbage. He looks up at me and says, 'There's some guy been looking for you since yesterday . . .'

'Who?'

'No fucking clue. He's not from the barrio. He's some rocker with a bunch of scars on his face.' Quique drops the cigarette butt, stamps it out and carries on, looking intrigued. 'Whoever the dude is, he's fucking weird. He says he's got a message for you from Toni.'

'And you haven't seen Toni around?' I ask, fumbling to get another cigarette out of the packet, but it's difficult because the cigarettes are trembling harder than the bullets earlier. At least this time I don't have to load them into a chamber. I'll be happy just to get one out of the pack. When I finally manage, I give the pack to Quique and he has no problem fishing one out. He's the one who gives me a light. I can't get the fucking lighter to work.

'I dunno, Gringo . . . I never met the guy.'

'Sure you met him, you just don't remember. You were a kid at the time . . .'

Quique stares at me and shrugs. He's right. Doesn't matter if he ever met Toni or not. I try to think, but I'm so parched I can't.

'So where is this guy?'

'At Zaid's place. I told him to wait for me there, said I'd try and track you down.'

'And how the fuck am I supposed to get there?' I ask, thinking about the litre of beer I'll neck soon as I get to the Turk's place.

'Long as you're sneaky and you don't go near the station, you'll be fine. Silva and Medusa have staked out the square in front of the station, they're not going to let this go . . . They're fucking psycho. Some of the kids said they're even looking for me.'

Quique heaves a sigh and lies back on the ground, arms folded behind his head. Closes his eyes. He's pale. He looks five or six years older. He looks like a plaster statue. Or a corpse.

'You look wrecked . . . You sleep?'

'A couple of hours, maybe.'

'Where did you spend the night?' I ask, putting my bag behind my head as a pillow and lying back.

'At Mamina's.'

'And you got in and out without anyone seeing?'

'Yeah, they fucked off sometime in the middle of the night. There was nothing happening and they got bored hanging round,' he explains.

'So did you see Mamina?'

'She didn't come back.' Quique clicks his tongue and curses under his breath. '. . . neither did my *mamá*.'

'You still worried about your sister?' I say, and I don't know why, but I think about the maggoty doll.

Quique opens his eyes, turns and flashes me a dirty look.

'You think?' he says and closes his eyes again, and I feel like a shit.

'Fuck you . . . how is this my fault?' I think, but I don't say it. For a while neither of us says anything. I listen to him breathing. Calm now. Like he's asleep. I can't sleep. The fear is eating me up inside.

'So what do we do, Gringo?' he asks unexpectedly, sitting up again.

'Well, I'm getting the fuck out of here. No way

I'm sticking around so they can cap me. You want to come with me, that's up to you.'

Quique opens his mouth. He hesitates. He looks at me, hard as stone.

'That's sweet, *loco*, that's cool. And how you planning to get gone? Take the four o'clock train?' he says. 'I mean, you could always ask Medusa and El Negrito to do you a solid, stop the 4.25 express. Throw a sleeper across the tracks like the railway workers did the day of the general strike and bye-bye. No, I've got a better idea . . . Why don't you walk to Zavaleta, ask one of Charly's boys to pay for a cab. What d'you think?' To rub it in, he gives me a serious look like he's expecting me to pick one of these options.

Turns out even Quique is taking the piss out of me now. The kid is frantic. And I don't blame him. If this shit is too much for me, it's a whole lot worse for him. Besides, I suppose maybe I sounded a bit harsh.

'I'll pay my own cab, *papá*. I've got more than enough cash,' I say, taking a fistful of bills from the bag. 'Here, go find Santi and give him this.' I make the big bills into a wad and hand it to him. It's a lot of cash, but I don't count it. If I can't buy my way out of this shit, I doubt I'll get a chance to splash the cash later.

Quique takes the money with kid gloves. Like there's shit on it, like he might catch scabies. A crumpled bill falls away. He picks it up and puts it with the others, never taking his eyes off me. Hardcore.

'Tell him to swing by the Turk's place at midnight. Tell him if he drives me down to Retiro in his Chevy, I'll give him the same again.'

Quique scratches his head. He digs his shoes into the ground. He's got them properly laced up now. Long laces tied twice around his ankles.

'He's not gonna give you a ride . . .' he says, and sighs like he's telling his kid sister there's no Santa Claus. 'The guy's shitting himself, there's no way he'd risk it. Charly's people know about the Chevy. Any suspicious move, he knows they'll end him. Besides, how can he take you if the road's blocked? There's a shitload of Feds at the crossroads outside Zavaleta, something about the teachers' strike or the unemployed . . . The whole thing's a clusterfuck . . .'

'So what? We go round by the refinery, or take the old road: if Santi's up for it, I don't see the problem. Just take him the money, tell him what I told you. What, you think he's chicken?'

'He won't do it, Gringo.'

'Just listen to me and stop bitching. I'm telling you, he'll be well up for it.'

Quique heaves a sigh, rubs his eyes. He's not convinced. Neither am I, but it's the only escape route I've got left.

'Go on, *loco*, make like the Duracell bunny and fuck off,' I say. 'Once we get to Retiro, we can swing by the children's hospital if you want. I know the way,' I lie, taking advantage of the fact his kid sister's sick. Keeping company with the local rats is clearly having an effect on me. All I need is a tail and I'd be one of them.

Quique looks at me for a second, then he says we might as well try and he leaves. I shout after him to give me a whistle if he spots anything dodgy on his way back to Zaid's place, and I wait. I wait too long, because Quique's warning never comes and, instead of getting my arse in gear, I sit there thinking about Chueco. And the arsehole who was tormenting me a while back shows up again and starts busting my balls. Before I realise, I'm talking to the dead like it was nothing weird.

'Be careful what you're doing,' I tell Chueco. 'Don't fuck up . . .'

FANTASY FICTION

'Oh, it's you. Yeah, I remember . . .' says Piti, one of Toni's friends. 'You showed up at Lezama Park the other day with a copy of *Moby Dick* under your arm . . .'

I agree with my eyes. A slight, slow blink. I've got my mouth full, my lips round the top of a bottle. And I can't nod, because I've got my head back so I can neck a litre of beer in one go.

It took him a minute before he recognised me. I had the advantage because I spotted him straight off. He's got the kind of face you don't forget in a hurry. Covered in scars and pockmarks. He's ugly as a hatful of arseholes.

'So? How's it going with the whale?'

'Piece of shit, that book,' I say, scanning the street. Suspicious.

No one's coming up from the river, and on the other side there's only a stray dog. I'm not the only one who's worried. Zaid the Turk is peering anxiously through the bars of his stall. All this shooting has finally shaken him out of his apathy, which means that fucking photo of his dog gets a break from having to deal with the weight of his guilt. At least this shit has done something positive – it's given Zaid something else to obsess about. I can't get my head round someone obsessing over a fucking photograph. I don't care if it's a photo of a missing kid or his mother who betrayed him. I feel sorry for the guy, because if he wants to throw a pity party, he doesn't need bad memories to do it. I don't do memories, good or bad. I can't be dealing with the past. But I'm being well and truly burned by the present. The fear, the dread, and all the beer in the world isn't going to put that fire out.

'What you saying, dude? *Moby Dick* is a complete fucking trip!' Piti says.

'It's a bunch of bullshit, and if you don't want to believe it, that's your problem.'

'Fuck sake, dude, you just don't get it!'

Piti looks at me smugly. He takes a swig of beer, hands me back the bottle and sparks up a cigarette. He studies me for a bit longer as he takes the first couple of puffs, then launches into a big lecture waving his cigarette like a pointer, like he's some professor. He gives me this whole spiel about the human condition, the hell of madness, the nature of evil and I don't know what all, and every couple of minutes he tells me that the whale doesn't really exist, that it's a metaphor for something that, if the whale didn't exist, would be nameless.

I let him ramble on, finish the beer and ask the Turk for another. The minute I see Piti's running out of steam, I cut in.

'You done?'

'More or less, *loco*, but I'm still not sure you get the book.'

'Metaphor my arse, you're the one who doesn't get it. All this horseshit is like some stoner tells you he's seen the face of the devil. It's bull . . . If someone really saw the devil, he wouldn't come out with shit about horns and hooves, nobody believes it. If he really saw the devil he'd wind up putting a bullet in his head or a needle in his arm, or he'd end up in a rubber room in some nuthouse.'

Piti pulls a face, gives me this smug smile. I go on talking so as not to end up smashing his fucking face.

'This whole story about the whale is a total crock too. We're supposed to believe anyone who goes after Moby Dick never comes back. So what about Ishmael? He was there and he came back, didn't he? The writer's a bullshit artist. He cheats. Far as I'm concerned, if it ended with Ishmael at the bottom of the sea with old Ahab, with the little fishies eating his eyes, it would have made more sense. If you're going to bullshit, at least make it convincing. Otherwise shut your arse.'

Piti lights another cigarette. He toys with the bottle, takes a couple of swigs, and tells me there's no way the plot of *Moby Dick* could turn out like that because that would be fantasy literature whereas Melville – that's the name of the guy who wrote the book, he reminds me – Melville's all about literary realism.

'Tell me something, professor,' I interrupt him. 'Did you come all this way to chat literature? Quit busting my balls about literary fucking realism.'

'Nuh-huh, dude,' he says gruffly. 'Toni sent me to give you a couple of messages.'

'Why didn't he come and tell me himself?'

'Ask him yourself, dude.' The guy clearly doesn't like being a messenger boy. And he sure as fuck doesn't like me reminding him he's one. 'Toni's waiting for you up in Zavaleta. Says not to believe the shit you've heard, says he had nothing to do with what happened to your old woman. Says you need to get the fuck out of the barrio asap. Charly's going to do a little ethnic cleansing, so there won't be much left standing.'

The air I'm breathing runs out of oxygen. I'm suffocating. The third gulp I take is a thick, smoggy hit that jolts my brain with a clarity I've never felt before. How the fuck does Toni know

I'm after him to find out about my mother? All I told him was Mamina wanted nothing to do with him and that if I was going to go work with him, I needed to know what had gone down between the two of them. He's hiding something. You start pleading innocent before you've been accused, you're fucking guilty. Right now, the last thing I want is to know what really went down. It doesn't matter any more.

It's not like we were really close, but Toni was always like a brother to me . . . Deliberately or not, he betrayed me, he left me in the lurch. Left me an orphan. Someone's got to pay for that.

The sudden fever I feel calms me and cranks me up. I'm dead. Just like Chueco.

'Tell him I can't go up there, because someone will cap me,' I say to Piti coolly. 'If he wants to get me out of this shit, he'll have to come down here.'

Piti stares at me incredulous and shrugs his shoulders.

'I can't see that happening, dude. Your people are a bit amped right now. Someone pulled a gun on me at the station. By some miracle, I got away with my shoes, but they took every peso I had. If that's how they treat strangers, I wouldn't like to imagine how they'd treat the prodigal son.' Piti finishes his beer, spits and concludes. 'Look, I've given you the message. If you like, I'll take a message back from you, but trust me on this, I don't think Toni's going to risk coming down here.'

I drag my bag up and sit on it next to Piti, spark up my nth cigarette and launch into an explanation. I'm calm, unruffled, like a good little boy who's just trying to come up with a solution that works for everyone. I explain to him the mess we're in, tell him there's nothing I can do, that he has to convince Toni to come down and mediate otherwise it's going to turn into a bloodbath. I explain there are women inside the bar, and at least one corpse. Rotting. I tell him that if Toni comes down unarmed, El Jetita will personally vouch for his safety. I explain about firing three shots in the air and waving a white flag. I tell him I'm going to be there too and I'm prepared to put myself on the line. I lie like a politician. I need to go through with this farce about divvying up the turf just so they'll stop shooting for a bit which will give me time to get the girls out the back and get the fuck out of here. After that, let them cap each other till there's no one left standing. It's the only way.

I sound completely reasonable. Just to make sure, I recap again, laying it on as thick as shit. I tell him Toni needs to get here asap. First thing in the morning latest because otherwise the people in the bar won't make it.

'Jesus, what a mess, dude,' Piti says to me. 'OK, I'll tell him.'

Now all I need is for Toni to believe it. I can't, even though the plan sounds completely reasonable. I can't because I'm already dead. I've snuffed it same as Chueco. Right now I'm blowing bubbles at the bottom of the ocean, slowly rotting away, just like Ishmael would be if his story was true.

SWEET DREAMS

Yani is sucking my cock. She's naked, kneeling. Like she's praying in front of an altar. Her mane of jet-black hair falls over her shoulders, curls shimmering blue in the sunlight. She arches her smooth back. I lean over and run my thumb down the ridged groove of her spine. I stop when I come to her arse. An inverted, fresh, mouth-watering summer pear, just waiting to be bitten. Beneath the blazing sun. She stops for a moment and smiles up at me. Her lips are moist. Oozing with the sweet nectar of the fruit. I'd like to taste them, but her face troubles me. It's not Yani now, but some other woman, a woman who seems familiar. She grips my cock with both hands and goes on sucking. She's good. She even plays with my balls. I'm just about to come when someone grabs my shoulder from behind and pulls me hard. Toni pushes me away. Suddenly I'm a kid again and he's towering above me. He glares down at me, a cigarette dangling from the corner of his mouth like a threat. He turns his back on me, starts fondling her tits, gives her arse a couple of slaps. I feel disgusted. When he's finished pawing her, he puts a leash around her neck and drags her away. Like she's some sort of animal. I'm left alone. I'm standing outside my school. The last teacher has gone home, they're closing the front gate and I know *mamá* is not coming to pick me up. That she'll never come and pick me up again. I fumble in the pocket of my school smock for change. I haven't got a peso. What do I do now? I feel fear and sadness course through me and I start crying, bawling at the top of my lungs.

I wake up choking on my own tears, my nose dripping snot, my face soaked. They're genuine tears. They broke out of my dream. The nightmare is not the one still echoing inside my head. The nightmare is waking up, because now I can't even go on crying to console myself. Even though the terror is the same. Maybe worse.

Night has fallen around me. It's cold. I'm still a little drunk. I fell asleep pressed against the bars of Zaid's stall, my neck at a right angle, now I've got a cramp. My mouth is parched. I get up and ask Zaid for some water. At least he's still here, like always. He gives me a bottle of mineral water. Cheap bastard always looking to make a sale. I only need something for my hangover. A glass of tap water would have done just as well. But I don't say anything. I give him the money, and I don't regret it. It's sweet, delicious. The problem now is that my stomach hurts. Hardly surprising, it's been at least twenty-four hours since I last had solid food. I ask Zaid if he'll make me a hamburger and he can't because he's out of gas. He offers me a sandwich instead. It's the last one. I stare at it under the filthy plastic cover that keeps the flies off. It turns my stomach but I say yes anyway. The bread's stale, the tomato tastes slightly rotten, I don't even taste the lettuce. I chuck it away because it's all slimy and wilted. But the meat is fucking awesome.

I stretch my legs, go and piss against a tree, come back and ask the Turk the time. It's nearly midnight. Santi should be showing up any minute now. In theory. Assuming Quique managed to track him down. Assuming he said he was up for driving me to Retiro, assuming he took the money. Assuming he didn't bottle out at the last minute, assuming Charly's people didn't get to him.

It's a lot of assuming, so I don't hold out much hope. Anyway, even if he does come, then what? I'm just going to fuck off and disappear? I don't even try to make the bastards pay for what they did to Chueco? I mean fuck sake, the guy was my *compañero*. And what if Santi shows without Quique? Am I going to do a runner and leave him stranded? And what about Yani? Didn't I tell her to wait for me, that I'd go back and get her?

Guilt starts eating away at my insides. Up to now, all I could think about was getting myself out of here and fuck everyone else. Look after number one. That's the law of the streets, what can you do? The question is whether I can get out of here. And I can. Otherwise why the fuck am I calmly waiting for Santi to show? So, what am I beating myself up about?

My head's spinning. I light one cigarette after another and still the *loco* doesn't show. Just as well, because I've still got to work out what to do. It's like a half-gutted cat hanging from a wall. Doesn't matter who killed it. That's beside the point. The point is what you do. You can fuck off out of there, but it won't bring the cat back and the body will still be there. You've got blood on your hands whatever you do. Blood and guts. But if you stay, you have to finish the job whether you like it or not. And to do that, you have to stick the knife in, whether you want to or not.

What I really don't want, I say to myself, is to lose it completely. It's getting colder and I can't stand still. I spark up the last cigarette in the pack and look over at the Turk who hasn't taken his eyes off me. Why doesn't he just go back to staring at the photo of his dog and leave me the fuck

alone? Maybe I was talking to myself again and
didn't realise it.

I go over to the bars, ask for a pack of cigarettes
and the Turk just stares at me.

'Why don't you go get some sleep, kid?
Whatever shit's going to happen is going to
happen,' he says. 'Right now with your bawling and
fretting and waiting for a miracle you're making
me nervous. Why don't you just get out of here?'

'And why don't you mind your own business and
stop busting my balls?'

Fucking retard usually can't string two words
together and when he finally does he gives me a
sermon . . .

He throws my change onto the little counter and
doesn't say anything. I scoop up the money and
he's still staring me in the eye. Coldly, now, his
eyes half closed. There's no defiance, no hatred in
those eyes. But there's no sympathy either. Fuck
knows what goes on in his head. The Turk's always
been unfathomable.

As is the night. It's pitch black. I haven't heard a
gunshot for a long while. And by now, it's obvious
Santi's not coming. It's pointless hanging around
waiting for him. But I stay a little longer, smoking
just for the sake of it. If it wasn't for the fact it's
only late summer, I'd swear it was freezing hard. I
pace up and down to keep warm and every time
I turn round, the Turk's still standing there staring

at me. Doesn't give up. Now he's starting to make me nervous. I've had enough. I pick up my bag, sling it over my shoulder and take my leave.

'See you tomorrow, Turk, sleep well,' I say, smiling politely and giving him the finger.

'Sweet dreams, Gringo,' he says and bursts out laughing.

Fuck him.

SUPPLIES AND MUNITIONS

The cart is full to bursting point. Car tyres, lumps of wood, cardboard boxes, iron bars and a trash can full of large bolts, screws and ball bearings. A handful of the fuckers weighs about a kilo. I put them back into the bucket and keep walking.

'Ammo for the catapults,' El Chelo explains, not that I asked. 'Things are getting heavy and we've got to be prepared. Didn't you have a glock?'

I feel a coldness in the small of my back where the gun's tucked into my belt. And that's where I'd like to leave it. I'm feeling like butter. I don't know if I'll be able to use it, but I nod anyway.

'Better bring it then, we'll need it,' he says.

One of the wheels gets stuck in the mud and the carts tips.

'Need a hand?' I say, gripping one side of the cart.

'No, leave it, you'll only fucking tip it over. Just give me a cigarette.'

While I take one out of the pack and light it for him, El Chelo pulls the cart out of the mud with a single jerk. He holds the cigarette carefully between two fingers like it's a spliff, or like his hands are greasy. He takes a deep drag. Blows out the smoke and stares at me, his head tilted back.

'So what you going to do now?'

'Don't know . . . Get the fuck out of here, I suppose.'

'Not got much choice, have you? I mean, after Chueco, you're next.' He raises an eyebrow. He's right. It's obvious.

El Chelo sticks the cigarette in a corner of his mouth so he can use both hands to pull the cart. At least he's heard. At least he knows. Saves me having to give him the news, him and the rest of Chueco's tribe. Or what's left of them. Something I'd rather avoid. How the fuck can I tell them what happened to Chueco when I hardly believe it myself?

'Why don't you come down the demo with me?' he says. 'Sooner or later the march is bound to head to the city centre. Because it's fucking pointless hanging around here. Then, when the coast's clear, you can bail if you want.'

Makes sense. The kid's doing my thinking for me. Must realise that at this point my head's not screwed on straight. El Chelo might come across as a loser, out with his cart sifting through trash, but it turns out the kid's cool. He's throwing me a lifeline and I didn't even ask.

'You seen Santi?' I ask.

'Disappeared off the face of the earth,' he says. 'Couldn't hack the pressure Charly's people were putting on him.'

And it's like he's making excuses for Santi. Some fucking friend he turned out to be. It's hardly the first time he's had someone pull a gun on him, and the guy didn't even stick around to find out the lie of the land. Just fucked off and left me and Chueco to fend for ourselves. Didn't think twice.

'What about Quique?'

'No clue,' he says.

Me neither. I've been wandering around making the call of a non-existent bird for fucking hours. But there's no answer.

'We're here,' El Chelo says, balancing one end of the cart on a mound so it doesn't tip over. 'Take the handle of the cart for me, I'll be right back.'

He nips into the shack where Chueco was living a couple of days ago. Not any more. He's in a different barrio now. It's not like I don't know the shack, I used to swing by here looking for him, I just hadn't realised we were headed that way. I was just trailing round after El Chelo like a dog, head in the clouds, not thinking about where we were going.

'You look like shit, Gringo.' El Chelo interrupts my thoughts. He's back already.

He shakes my shoulder with his free hand. The other hand is holding a bunch of worn-out blankets he brought from inside. He stuffs them into the cart as best he can. They look pitiful. They're filthy and torn, with more holes than blanket . . . They're fucking pitiful.

'Probably be a long night . . . These blankets are for the old women,' he explains, 'and for the kids when they get cold. Don't know why the fuck people are bringing kids on the march, but I guess they've nowhere to leave them . . .'

He's talking to himself, I've stopped listening. He's fucking pitiful himself. He's taking this whole thing serious. He's passionate about it. Passion is all he's got left. Everything else is piled into this cart. If he could see himself the way I see him . . . But he doesn't need to, because he sees me through his eyes and it's the same thing. I'm guessing I look pretty fucking pitiful myself. Standing here in the dark like a spare prick at a whore's wedding. Fucking borderline psychotic and not saying a word. But even that's not right. It's not about us, it's this whole situation that's fucking pitiful. The night itself is wretched and the barrio is just a gaping hole of misery and fear in the dawn light.

'Right, I'm heading off,' he says when he's

finished repacking his load. 'Hang out here for a bit if you like, Gringo, it's no sweat.' As he says it, he jerks his head towards the door, and pushes me gently. Like I might not understand the words. I must really be fucked up. I give him a wink and thank him by offering him a couple of cigarettes. It's not like anyone ever needed an invite to crash in this crackhouse before. The fact Chelo feels he has to issue one says a lot.

I watch him trundle off with his cart, then I go inside. The stench hits me like a fist and, weird as it sounds, it clears my head. It's a pungent mix of urine, vomit, sweat and years of built-up filth. Inside is dark, but I don't waste time looking for a light switch, even assuming there was a working light bulb. By the time I'm a couple of steps inside, my eyes have adjusted to the gloom. Old man Soria is slumped on the table, a carton of cheap wine within easy reach. In a low voice he drivels drunkenly, an interminable litany of threats, curses and prayers. They broke his nose. It's swollen and purple as an aubergine. A trail of dried blood runs all the way down his chest. At least I now know where the stink is coming from. The old man's pissed himself and thrown up all down one side of his body.

Against the tin wall, someone shifts on a straw mattress. From outside comes the rustle of the trees shaking in the breeze. Nothing else. Ever since

I had that nap at Zaid's place, I haven't heard a single shot. This dubious silence is enough to drive you mad. It scares me shitless.

The silence seeps in from outside, but inside is a symphony of murmurs. The old man saying his rosary is joined by the whimpers and sighs of the body on the mattress. I wander over and one eye stares up at me, blazing like a white-hot coal. The other is swollen shut. A hand flies out and grabs my shoulder.

'Gimme something, Gringo,' a voice stammers. 'Whatever you got. I can't fucking take it any more.' The plea comes as a feeble murmur from lips that are bruised and split in several places, but the hand grips my shoulder hard. It takes me a second to recognise the face behind this mask. They really did Willi over. His own mother wouldn't recognise him, if he had a mother.

'Don't have anything, champ,' I say, pulling his hand off me.

The guy is soaked to the skin. He's sweating like a pig, he's dehydrating. He's in withdrawal, going cold turkey from the pills, the *merca*, the acid or whatever the fuck he's been putting in his body. He's the first casualty of the war between Charly and El Jetita. The war between suppliers has left him with no supplies. And right now, he's in hell.

That makes two of us, though at least my hell

isn't chemical, unlike his. And the body is implacable. The body gives the orders, I think. Then I remember that I still have a small lump of the weed we robbed from Medusa and Silva.

'Actually, I have got a bit of weed, Willi,' I say. 'Give me some skins and I'll roll up.'

The guy leans up on one elbow, desperate, rummaging through his pockets. He pulls out a crumpled cigarette paper. I smooth it with my fingers and notice that the edge is damp. The *loco*'s even sweating from his fingertips. He's practically in a coma. I crumble the weed quickly, take out the seeds so it burns properly. When I start rolling, the paper comes apart in my hand. If I ask him for another skin, he'll only make it wet and that'll get us nowhere.

I open my bag, take out the whale book and rip out a page. It's smooth and thinner than the rolling paper. It's perfect. I tip all of the weed on to the paper and roll it using both hands. It's not a spliff, it's a fucking Cuban cigar. It looks like one of those huge blunts Bob Marley used to smoke. I spark it, take a couple of tokes and pass it to Willi. Now the gleam in his one good eye has a partner, a burning coal in the darkness. The guy tokes on it hard and fast, not taking it from his bruised lips. He smokes like a fucking chimney.

The weed chills me out a bit. My thoughts become fuzzy. I'm guessing it does the same for

Willi, because he's not shaking any more. Or whimpering.

'Thanks, Gringo, you're a god, you're fucking Gardel.'

Yeah, Gardel. The plane crash. Like a dog, I look for a corner where I can curl up for a bit. I find a large burlap sack. Old Soria's mumbling sends me off to sleep. Top-class fucking weed, has to be, because now this shithole smells of jasmine.

BACK IN BLACK

Before it gets light, I leave the shack, moving quickly, pressing ahead like I've got somewhere I've got to be, like I've got someone waiting for me. But neither of those things is true. Truth is, I'm no one, I'm nothing, an empty space. So I wander in circles around the barrio in the dawn's early light. Panicked. And what's really freaking me out is how quiet it is. There's not a soul around. It's like I'm a ghost in a ghost town.

The only sign of life – and even that's barely a murmur – comes from Fat Farías's place. A sound so faint that – given the distance – I'm not sure if it's real or if I'm imagining it. I want to go closer, but I don't dare. I see two figures coming down the alley that leads to the station. Hand in hand. They're about the same height, both dressed in black. They don't say a word. I can't be sure, so I hide behind the skeleton of a clapped-out car and wait.

'Where are you headed, Grandma?' I emerge
from my hiding place when I see her.

'*M'hijo!* You gave me such a fright . . .' Mamina
says.

I recognised her in the distance from her
clothes. I didn't recognise Quique. He looks
different. He's wearing his hair gelled down, a
white shirt and a black jacket and trousers. He's
even wearing shoes. He looks perfect, like he's
making his First Communion. Mamina's a crafty
old dear. God knows where she got the cash to
dress him up like that. I stand there
dumbfounded, I don't get it.

'We're going to the church, for his sister's . . .'
Mamina can't bring herself to finish the
sentence.

'Oh, Jesus . . . Oh shit, I'm really sorry, *loco*,' I
say to Quique and hug him hard.

I have to fill the silence, but the minute I open
my mouth I regret it. Just words. He stands there
like a stone. Stock-still. He doesn't react. He barely
moves his eyes, huge and round as the day that's
dawning. They flit wetly from one thing to
another as though unable to make sense of the
world. He doesn't even seem to recognise me. He's
staring into the distance, towards a horizon that
isn't there.

'And where are you off to with that bag?'
Mamina asks.

'Wherever . . .' I say. 'If I stay here in the barrio, they're going to kill me.'

'Have you seen the way they've wrecked the house? Didn't I tell you not to get mixed up with those people? What do I have to do to get through that thick skull of yours?' Mamina scolds me. But it's a waste of breath, there's no way to fix this now.

'I'm sorry, *abuela*,' I say, staring at the ground like I used to when I was a kid.

But I know that it's too late for apologies. You can't put things right just like that . . .

Mamina pinches my cheek roughly and gives me a slap. She slaps me hard, but with love.

'You're like Antonio. You get mixed up with a bad crowd, get involved in all sorts. You're going to end up just like him.'

There she goes again. But I've had it up to here with her hints and insinuations.

'What the fuck did Toni ever do to you, Mamina?' I explode. 'Just give it to me straight, because he's back here in the barrio.'

'To me? Nothing. It was what he did to you. Don't you remember?' she answers in a whisper. Sweet and gentle as ever. I bite my lip, ball my fists, my eyes blazing. 'No, obviously you don't want to remember,' she goes on. 'You don't remember how he seduced your mother, how he took her off to Zavaleta and made her work as a prostitute . . . ? It's his fault that Cecilia wound up in a ditch, and that's something I can never forgive him for.'

Cecilia. *Mamá*'s name. I haven't heard it in years. Cecilia. Now it's just an empty word. Hollow. But it echoes inside me. I count: one, two, three . . . seven letters. Together they spell out something I've forgotten, then suddenly something clicks. And I remember. Inside my head, the images rain down like blows. Toni flirting with her as she hung out the washing and *mamá* laughing. I remember that he always used to say to her, 'You're only starving to death because you want to, Cecilia.' I remember them whispering together in the street . . . And I remember a shape wrapped in a blanket lying on the hard shoulder next to a police car and Mamina pulling me away so I wouldn't see . . .

'You're all grown up now, Gringuito, you're your own man. If you need to leave the barrio, then leave . . . But if you go, that's an end of it. Don't come back crying to me,' Mamina whispers and the look of scorn on her face unnerves me.

'Don't worry, *abuela*, I know what I have to do,' I say defiantly, but I can feel my heart sink.

'Come on, your mother's all on her own keeping

vigil over your sister,' she says to Quique, but she's looking at me.

'Hang in there, *loco*,' I say, squeezing his arm. 'You need to stay strong, to support your mother.'

Quique nods at me and blinks. He stays strong. But on the inside, he's shattered. He takes Mamina's arm and calmly leads her away. As if it were true, as if Quique, in his First Communion suit, is the one who has to support Mamina. But it's the other way round. Quique's the one who's about to commune with death. You might see the signs, but you never know when to expect it. Like with Chueco, taking communion from the Grim Reaper. I was the altar boy. The communion wafer was a bullet.

If there's one out there for me, let it come now, without warning, because I've had about as much of this shit as I can take. Now the sun is tracing everything in yellow gold. Like it's all new. The puddles, the line of shacks, the rubbish bags ripped open by the dogs, the far end of the street, Mamina's shoulders and Quique's dark hair framed against the sunlight . . . Every outline shimmers as though something is about to happen, as though somehow it might be possible to start over.

Cloudless. The clear morning sky greets the sound of bells. The call to Mass, a thankless,

224

never-ending funeral. But it's not the church bells ringing out, but shots. I can hear them clearly. Three bullet wounds in the silence of the dawn sky. It's the signal.

UNDERWATER

The signal sets me off and I run. I run heedlessly towards Fat Farías's bar. But I'm not seeing straight. I overshoot by a couple of blocks. I head towards the rear of the bar. To the side gate that leads into the little yard. I could have come through the neighbour's yard on the far side of the block and vaulted the low wall, the way Chueco and I got out last time, but there's no point. If there's a bullet out there with my name on it, I'd rather it came now.

I'm confused by the clamour of voices. I can't make out what they're saying. Just overlapping voices, shouts and threats and swearing. The voices are coming from outside and inside the bar. It sounds like they're negotiating the terms of the ceasefire before starting negotiations. On the building site opposite, a white flag is waving between the rifles pointed at the sky. Though it's not actually white. It's a San Lorenzo football shirt.

Blue and red. Like the one Toni used to wear every Sunday when he went to the match. I can't believe it. It's got to be him. He's doing all this so he can go inside. Everything's turning out just exactly the way El Jetita wanted it.

I push the gate and go inside, only to have an Itaca aimed at me through the half-open kitchen door, the twin barrels like two eyes staring into mine.

'Chill, it's just Gringo,' I shout to Robledo, though all I can see is his huge moustache peeking out over the barrel.

The *milico* lowers the gun, pops his head round the door and says, 'Are you fucked in the head? How the hell did you get here? What d'you want?'

I don't bother to reply, partly because I can't think of anything to say.

'Get in here, kid. You can stand guard, I'm going out front,' Robledo says and disappears.

I head towards the kitchen, but as I cross the yard, I hear someone sobbing over the shouting from the bar. It takes a second for me to work out the crying is coming from the storage shed in the yard. I have a sudden, sick feeling, like a rock in the pit of my stomach. It's Pampita, they beat her up . . . They fucked her over . . . I open the door. But it's not Pampita I see lying there, whimpering, cursing, bare legs flailing, rolling over and fumbling as though trying to turn off the light streaming in through the open door. It's Yanina. Pampita is kneeling next to her, holding her, trying to comfort her, whispering something into her ear, something that sounds like a lullaby, only in Aymara or in Quechua, as she waves for me to go away.

'What's wrong? What's wrong, Yani?' I ask like a fucking moron. After all it doesn't take much imagination to work it out. But obviously my imagination has failed me, because when I try to take her by the shoulders she screams hysterically. She's completely lost it.

'You cunt, you fucking cunt!' she screams at me, digging her nails into my face like I was to blame for this. The unkempt hair, the swollen eyes, the bleeding lip, the bruise on her cheek. As though I'm to blame for what I can see through the nails clawing at me.

'Leave her, Gringo, leave her . . .' Pampita says, holding Yanina's arms.

'Who the fuck did this? Who?' I say, but I don't let go.

She struggles like a wild animal, howls and screams and kicks out at me. She's out of control.

'Get the fuck out of here, now,' Pampita shouts, but now she's struggling with me, trying to get my hands away from Yanina's shoulders. They must be burning her because her shoulders are freezing.

'Who the fuck did this?' I scream but neither of them answer.

'Get out, you prick! Can't you see? The damage is done!' Pampita roars, so close to me I can feel her breath against my cheek.

And suddenly I'm calm. The rage in her eyes leaves me dumbfounded. I would never have thought I could see such hatred in those eyes. Pampita's eyes, because Yanina's eyes don't see anything. They're expressionless, in spite of her tears.

'Leave her in peace, will you?' she says, waving for me to leave again. Yani's howls subside into ragged, wrenching sobs. She's just a weeping machine now. And Pampita's arms go round her again, rocking her, trying to calm her.

I get up from the straw mattress as though I understand everything. But there's nothing to understand. I leave without a sound. I gently close the door of the shed, leaving it ajar just like it was, and find myself holding the .38 in my right hand. At what point did I take it out? It's a mystery. Because I was carrying it in my belt, in the small of my back, that I do know. I slowly creep towards the kitchen door. I put my head inside and scan the room, but I can't make out anything. It's dark. What little light there is filters through the strip curtain from the bar. The shouting is over. I hear a gurgling sound and see Fat Farías lying next to one of the fridges. He's choking on his own blood. Someone smashed his face in again, but this time it wasn't me. I hear whispers of conversation from the bar, but that's all. I wait a couple of seconds until I hear El Jetita shout across the street.

'Come on, *loco*, get over here. Come on, we need to talk!'

I creep back to the gate and step outside. The puddles and the wet street shimmer. The sun by now is some way over the horizon. Behind the half-finished wall on the building site opposite, the shotguns are still pointed towards the sky. They're quivering nervously. The white flag – the football shirt – is gone. Toni is wearing it now, walking slowly but surely, crossing the junction diagonally. He's staring straight ahead of him. He's empty-handed.

I raise my gun and aim at the red-and-blue stripes. But my hand is shaking. And by the time I aim again, it's too late. I miss. The shot whistles up the street. Time slows to a crawl. Every movement becomes viscous, it's like the whole barrio is at the bottom of the sea.

I see Toni's look of surprise. His eyebrows shoot up, his mouth drops open. The barrels of the shotguns slowly return to the horizontal. Toni bends down, lifts the cuff of his jeans and takes out the gat he's got tucked into his sock. A gun fires from the building site. Toni raises his own weapon and takes a bullet to the chest. He freezes for an instant, jolted by the bullet and, his hand still hovering in the air, he fires. The red stain blossoming on his striped shirt gradually spreads. And the shots keep coming, one after another. Toni is hit by three more stray rounds. In the knee, the shoulder and one right in the middle of his forehead. His head jerks back. And still it takes an eternity for him to fall. Then finally he sinks to the ground as though crushed beneath the weight of the water.

Shots multiply, almost overlapping, but not quite, I can clearly hear each one. I kick open the gate and am unsettled by how slow my own movements seem.

I start running, and every step I take is a feat. I have to persuade each muscle to react before it moves. And when it does, it is only to meet the resistance of gallons and gallons of water. I'm five thousands metres underwater. At such a depth, no sunlight filters through and I have to retrace my steps from memory. Along the way, I feel the direction of the fissure as the clamour of voices and gunfire gradually fades into the gloom of the marine trench. If I had flippers, I'd be able to move faster, I think to myself, as I watch my knees rise and fall. The problem is breathing, because no matter how wide I open my mouth, no air comes in. Only water, I swallow huge quantities. More salty than tears. More bitter than guilt. I'm drowning.

THE RED WHALE

I'm gasping by the time I get to the bridge, my mouth opening and closing like a fish out of water, but I don't stop running until I reach the front of the demo. I sprint the last hundred metres. El Chelo appears out of the crowd, a smile on his face.

'You made it, I knew you would . . .'

I want to say something but I can't get the words out. I'm still panicked. I nod my head and raise my arms trying to get air into my lungs. I interlink my fingers at the back of my neck and stand there, elbows flailing, gasping for breath.

'They're really fucking going for it, huh?' El Chelo says, jerking his head back towards the barrio. 'When the wind's blowing this way, you can hear the gunshots even over all the noise we're making here . . .' He stares into the distance, at some indeterminate point between the station and Fat Farías's bar.

I'm not surprised, it's not like it's that far. We're

only about thirty or forty blocks from the shoot-out. But I feel as though I've been running for miles, for years. Three or four at least, before I reached the last truck in the traffic jam, and a couple more from the corner by the refinery to here, at the front of the march. I feel I've aged seven or eight years during that run.

'It's only when they stop shooting that we've got to worry –'

I cut him short.

'Any moment now, it can't go on much longer . . .'

'Yeah, figures. We'll have to be on the lookout, because when Charly's people start heading back to Zavaleta, the Feds with them are going to try and infiltrate the march,' El Chelo says. 'I've already given Toro Lopéz the heads-up – he's in charge of the demo, but everyone needs to keep their eyes open, otherwise they'll fuck us over. It's one thing facing the Feds head-on, but if we've got them coming at us from behind, that's very fucking different,' he explains, pointing at the *milicos* up ahead like he's a tourist guide.

The police cordon isn't exactly much: three squad cars blocking the road about a hundred metres away and half a dozen Feds goofing around. Behind them is a blue riot truck that could be a water cannon or a prison bus, can't tell from this distance.

'This is no fucking joke, Gringo,' El Chelo says, like he can read my thoughts. 'They're sending in the army, they've just announced it on the radio.'

'Yeah, but they'd need a fucking regiment to take on all the marchers,' I say, looking out over the sea of people and trucks. The whole barrio is out. A column of smoke is rising from the road, thick as tar, and the local kids are still stoking the fire. Among the kids chucking rubbish onto the burning car tyres I recognise a couple of faces from Quique's neighbourhood. He'd probably be doing exactly the same if it weren't for the fact that he's dressed in his Sunday best, burying his kid sister.

Behind the pall of smoke is a sea of placards and makeshift cardboard signs. The deafening hammering of drums and saucepans never stops. The teachers are the ones most worked up, it's obvious from the school smocks fluttering everywhere. The council workers seem more relaxed. Some of them are even chatting to the unemployed, who are all wearing red wristbands to identify themselves. They're by far the majority. The rest are labourers of various sorts, I can't really tell who they are, though I recognise the faces. They're all from the barrio, that I do know. There's all sorts, from wheeler-dealers and layabouts to construction workers and industrial machine workers.

There's several groups gathered around the truck at the front of the march. Some drinking *mate*, others playing *truco* on upturned empty crates. I figure they're truck drivers, and they're taking this whole thing in their stride. They're stranded because either the cargo they're hauling or their rigs are too big to turn them round. So there's fuck all they can do.

All along one side of the road is a string of tents, some canvas, some plastic, some made out of blankets. It's like an Indian village: old women, kids and babies. There's a patch of ground with three or four bonfires and a bunch of big steaming pots. And I'm praying that they're for everyone, because I'm fucking starving.

'You think they won't take us on?' El Chelo's comment comes after a delay, as though he too has been surveying the scene. 'They'll send a whole regiment, two if they need to . . .'

He's laying it on thick. Very thick. I give a mocking whistle and stare into the distance like I can see the cavalry riding to the rescue.

'You've got no clue what's about to go down here,' he says.

I spark up a cigarette and El Chelo's eyes shine. I offer him one before he can ask. With the first drag, he says, 'I guess you brought the strap?'

'You guess right . . .' I say, putting down the bag I've had slung over my shoulder for an eternity. It doesn't weigh much, but my shoulder and the back of my neck are rubbed raw.

'Well, at least that's one more . . . I mean, with all the people here, you could count the number of guns on the fingers of one hand.'

'What do you expect? They're working stiffs.'

'Yeah, I know, *viejo*, but it's not like they thought they were coming on a fucking picnic,' El Chelo says and he's right. Well, partly right.

'You carrying?'

'No.'

'So what the fuck you bitching about?' I say. El Chelo glares at me, but he doesn't say anything. 'Here, take this,' I say, handing him the .38.

The guy's eyes widen in surprise. He can't bring himself to touch it.

'Straight up, Gringo?' he insists. 'You're actually giving this to me?'

'Call it a loan. If I need it back, I'll ask for it,' I say, and this seems to do the job, because El Chelo relaxes.

'Safe, thanks,' he says finally, taking the strap.

I chuck him the box of cartridges too, without warning, but El Chelo's got good reflexes. He catches it. He seems really touched. He pats me on the back, gives me a man-hug. Any minute now and he'll start in with the kisses. I see it coming and push my way through the crowd, looking for somewhere to put down my bag. El Chelo sticks to

237

me like a shadow, blethering on, saying the first
thing that comes into his head. Excitement has set
his tongue loose.

We've wandered a few metres, zigzagging
through the crowd, when I hear a voice I recognise
shouting behind me.

'Hey, if it isn't Captain Ahab himself!'

I turn and there's Piti holding a bottle of beer.
He's babbling on to a girl in a Rasta hat and some
skinny guy in a khaki shirt in a crowd of about a
dozen people. All from outside the barrio. The
same guys I ran into in the city centre a week ago
– the Students' Union militants who were marching
down the Avenida Corrientes with no one bringing
up the rear. They don't need a banner, anyone
could pick them out a mile off. Rich, middle-class
kids from the posh suburbs of Buenos Aires
coming into town to play at being revolutionaries.

'You find your white whale yet, Captain?' Piti
shouts over, holding up the bottle in a salute. He
hands the beer to the girl in the Rasta hat and
whispers something to the rest of the gang. It must
be funny, because they're all shitting themselves
laughing. He's taking the piss out of me.

I walk over to the group, itching to break his
face. 'You know that *loco*?' El Chelo asks.

I nod my head, fist balled by my side. I look the
kids up and down, give them the evils, but they
don't seem intimidated. Quite the opposite.

'Haven't found it yet,' I say to Piti, 'but I'm still looking! What about you?'

'Too right, *viejo*, only mine's not a whale . . . more of a mermaid with great tits.' He glances at his girl who gives him a disgusted look and swears under her breath. 'A siren from the coast of Jamaica more dangerous than anything Odysseus had to face.'

The rest of the students are whispering and laughing, and I'm guessing Piti's not the butt of their jokes.

'Mind telling me what the fuck your friends are laughing at?' I say, jabbing a finger into Piti's chest. 'Someone could get the wrong idea. They need to realise they're not in some nice middle-class suburb and to stop taking the piss . . .'

'Come on, Gringo,' El Chelo says, tugging on my arm. 'Leave it, don't start something . . .'

'My friends?' Piti sighs. 'Yeah . . . I wish the fuck they'd drink beer and stop reciting *Das Kapital*, they're busting my balls here . . .' He's refusing to be wound up, trying to play the peacemaker. The kids all cheer him on. Not me.

'Chill, *compañero* . . .' the guy in the khaki shirt says. 'The enemy's over there . . .' He points at the police cordon and offers me the beer.

'So what's up, you Bollinger Bolshevik?' I say, taking a long slug of beer. I can be a smart-arse too when I want.

'Hey . . . take it easy, *loco*, it's all good . . . We were just laughing because Piti here says you think Melville was wrong . . . But don't get mad . . .'

'Ignore them,' says the guy with glasses, the guy who was barking orders into the megaphone on last week's demo. 'I'm with you on this one . . .' he says, patting me on the back and I'm wondering what the fuck gives him the right to be so buddy-buddy. 'Melville's a decadent writer. His vision of society doesn't go beyond his own bourgeois, conservative, late-nineteenth-century ideology. The only thing he's got going for him is he points up the excesses of rampant capitalism . . . *Moby Dick* describes the foundering of a whole society, of a system of production based on authoritarianism. And *Bartleby, the Scrivener* – you read that?' I shake my head, but the kid just carries on with his lecture. 'Well, it's not exactly a masterpiece, and it's really short, but it's good because it shows how capitalist alienation suffocates even the smallest revolutionary reflex. But Melville doesn't really question anything, he's not offering any solutions . . .'

This guy has clearly found his whale, I think, while he blethers on, waving his hands like a fucking lunatic. Only his isn't white, it's red. The colour of the proletarian revolution. But the guy hasn't a fucking clue . . . If he had, he wouldn't come looking for it up here in this shithole, and he certainly wouldn't be lecturing the locals. Is he looking to get his head busted? Because if he wants to go down with his whale, I'd be happy to help. Right now I'd happily kill the fucker with my bare hands.

And his friends are just the same – can't open their mouths without putting a foot in it. They gather round the guy in the glasses and start debating points of order. Piti makes the most of this to chat to the girl with the Rasta cap and the tits. Whispering in her ear. He's hitting on her, and it must be working, because she's smiling at him.

'Gringo! Come here a second!' shouts El Chelo, who's wandered away from the group. Crafty fucker. He's calling me over because he knows if I hang with these kids any longer, things are going to kick off.

IN A CIVILISED FASHION

On a full belly, everything looks different. Worse. Even the perky little old ladies scraping out their pots to serve a last helping to the stragglers make me depressed. Despite the fact that the food seems to have lifted everyone's spirits. Everyone is in a better mood, you can tell. They're chatting and laughing, someone's playing the guitar, and people are passing *mate* around.

El Chelo's on the cadge for a cigarette to help his digestion. I give him one and spark up one for myself. Without saying anything, I get up and go over to give back the crockery some woman lent us so we could eat – a saucepan lid, a disposable plastic tray and a couple of spoons. She's sitting in the shade of a makeshift tent, breastfeeding her kid. When she sees me coming over, she covers herself as best she can and shouts, 'Just leave them there!'

I say thanks and turn away so as not to embarrass

her. I skirt round a gang of kids kicking a plastic bottle and, passing the bonfire, I chuck my cigarette butt into the flames. The wind shifts every now and then. The thick greasy smoke whirls and eddies. It stings my nose.

'You want me to introduce you to El Toro López?' says El Chelo, who's leaning against one wheel of his cart. 'He's over there, the dark guy in the cap talking to that group of unemployed guys, see him?' He points.

'No way.'

'Why not? He's a good guy . . .' El Chelo says, a little pissed off.

'I don't care, I don't want anything to do with leaders. Far as I'm concerned, they can all go fuck themselves . . .'

'Whatever you want, *loco*. Just saying.'

We don't say anything for a while and I feel embarrassed. Embarrassed for him. Maybe I hurt his feelings. I was a bit harsh. I stand up and, without saying anything, I clap him on the back. El Chelo looks up, gives me a wink. We're cool.

I wander around, killing time, bored out of my skull, keeping my ears open . . . I don't talk to anyone. I go over to where the truckers are playing cards and, since I've got a wad of cash, they deal me in to their game of *truco*. We lose three hands straight. The fat guy partnering me looks like he wants to cap me. He hasn't had a single decent card for a while and he blames me for it. Says I'm bad luck, says he was on a roll until he was partnered with me. Since the fat guy's pissing me off by now, I bail. I tell the old guy he's been sneaking a look at my cards and I fuck off.

The sun is slipping behind the horizon. The sky bleeds red and purple and the air becomes heavy and charged with unease. The sort of electrical charge that builds up before a storm. I see the López guy anxiously pacing among the demonstrators, giving out orders, I can tell from the signals he's making. The teachers are all grouped together, a tight knot of white smocks; they're probably wondering what the hell they're going to do if all this kicks off. Makes sense, they're all about books and blackboards, what the fuck do they know about bullets and tear gas?

'Here come the Feds,' El Chelo warns me.

We watch, fascinated, as the *milicos* climb out of their trucks. A bunch of them form a cordon with riot shields in front of the patrol cars and the rest of them pile in behind. They're a tight group, the only things visible above the riot shields, their helmets and their semi-automatics.

Things don't seem quite so organised our end, but they're getting there. Anyone not feeding the bonfire is collecting rocks and stones to throw. Chains and knives start to appear and a couple of guns. El Chelo hands out the bolts and ball bearings to anyone with a catapult. I see him in the crowd a few metres away, taking out the .38, putting bullets in the chamber. He looks up and our eyes meet. He gives me a thumbs up. I do the same just as the cop with the megaphone orders us to disband. 'Clear the road now in a civilised fashion, before the operation commences,' the *milico* says. I recognise the voice. It's the guy I heard talking to El Jetita on the police radio the other night. Commissioner *hijo-de*-fucking-*puta* Zanetti. And that phrase, 'in a civilised fashion,' reminds me of what Chueco said the other day about there being seven ways to kill a cat, but when it comes down to it, there are only two that matter: in a civilised fashion, or like a fucking savage.

And so, in a civilised fashion, we stand our ground. The teachers start up with the national anthem and everyone in the crowd joins in. At the end, there's a burst of applause, of cheers and whistles like we're all celebrating coming top of the league. But we didn't. We're being hammered. After the last cheers, a gulf of fear opens and the *milicos* make the most of the silence to start their advance. With every step, the thud of marching boots gets louder. They're heading straight for us.

In the faces of the people nearest me, I see everything: rage, fear, panic, dread . . . I look around for El Chelo but find myself face to face with the kid in the glasses. He's bricking it, it's obvious. The kid backs away and finally I see El Chelo who's looking at me grimly.

'Fuck sake, come on!' he roars, waving the gat.

I pick up a stone and hurl it; the first shot rings out. It's raining tear gas. We throw anything we can find at them, including the smoking canisters of tear gas. Now things are really kicking off. In a seriously civilised fashion . . .

www.vintage-books.co.uk